MW00527556

Also by Justin M. Woodward:

The Variant
Candy
Rotten Little Things

ACKNOWLEDGEMENTS

Before I show my appreciation for all the help I have received since the completion of *The Variant* and the completion of the book you're about to begin, I feel compelled to ask you, the reader, to do yourself a favor (if you haven't already) and read *The Variant* first. I can't tell you why, but you'll be glad you did by the end of this book.

Now, where to begin? Of course, there are some people I'd like to thank for specific reasons which I can't list without spoilers, and so, those people will be thanked after the main story in the 'From the Author' section. For now, however, I have plenty of others to thank.

Thank you to my amazing wife, Alison, for putting eyes on the first draft and offering your opinions and suggestions.

Thank you to Judy Haigh, Melissa Lucas, and Christina Arico for being my beta-readers on this one, trust me when I say your feedback means the world to me.

Thank you, James Newman for taking the time to write a foreword for this book, you're amazing. Thank you to fellow author, Duncan Ralston, for the kind words, and to fellow author, J. Z. Foster, for taking a hard look at the book and offering what I consider to be invaluable advice and perspective. Special thanks to RJ Roles.

Thank you to the band Other Lives, who I borrowed the name *Tamer Animals* from, and who graciously gave me permission to borrow the name. I highly recommend their album of the same name.

Thank you, François Vaillancourt, for coming through with some absolutely gorgeous cover art, you nailed it. Thank you to Pete Kahle, I'm grateful for everything.

And thank you, for buying this book. I hope it speaks to you in one way or another.

- *Justin*

TAMER ANIMALS

By Justin M. Woodward

Copyright © 2019 by Justin M. Woodward and simple bicycle publishing. Originally published in 2018 by Bloodshot Books.

All Rights Reserved.

No part of this book may be reproduced, distributed or transmitted in any form or by any means without the author's written consent, except for the purposes of review

Cover Design © 2018 by François Vaillancourt

ISBN-13: 978-0-9979409-2-3

This book is a work of fiction. Names, characters, places and incidents are either a product of the author's fertile imagination or are used fictitiously. Any resemblance to actual events, places or persons, living or dead, is entirely coincidental.

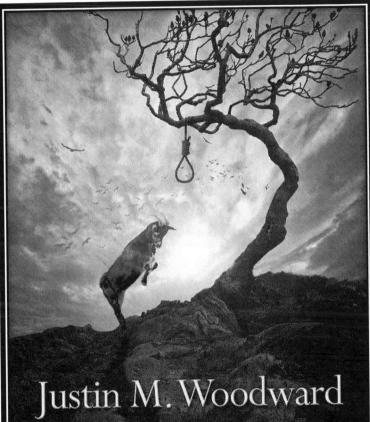

Justin M. Woodward

TAMER
ANIMALS

For Alison,

for taking the journey with me.

FOREWORD

So, apparently I have become the go-to guy for blurbing and writing Forewords (yeah, I know the former isn't a word, I just made that up, but it works so we'll go with it) for tales that fall within the "coming-of-age" genre. I have written a few of coming-of-age books of my own – starting with my first novel, *Midnight Rain*, and followed since by *Odd Man Out* and the just-released *Dog Days o' Summer* (co-written with Mark Allan Gunnells) – and from what I can tell readers dig them quite a bit. In fact, the consensus seems to be that this makes me some kind of expert on this thing called "coming-of-age."

Whatever. I'll be the first to tell you that I'm not an expert on ANYTHING. Okay, maybe I've got a real talent for picking my nose when no one's looking, or wasting time on Facebook when I should be writing (just ask my wife), and I swear to God I can carry a tune if I'm alone in my car with the windows rolled up . . . but that's about it.

Here's the thing, though: I do know good writing. And I know what makes a story work so well that readers are unable to put it down, no matter what genre it might fall into.

I know when I've read something that makes me not only proud to endorse it, but excited to tell everyone I know that they should read it too, as soon as possible.

The book you hold in your hands, it's that kind of gem.

It's the kind of book that made me happy to tell its author "Hell, yeah, I'll write a foreword for ya" almost before he had finished asking the question.

I'm ashamed to admit that I haven't read anything else by Justin, despite the fact that this young writer has several published works to his name. *Tamer Animals* was the first, but it definitely won't be the last.

When Justin contacted me about this, and told me a bit about his upcoming novel, he barely had to say anything more than "it's like *The Texas Chainsaw Massacre* meets *Stand By Me*." I was instantly sold with that pitch. *Tamer Animals* sounded like the greatest thing ever!

Turns out this comparison wasn't at all off-base.

Tamer Animals stands toe-to-toe with many of my favorite coming-of-age books and movies. It's about the wonders of growing up as well as the fears that come with it; it's about the thrill that comes from doing stuff we're not supposed to do, and of the consequences that come from too much of a good thing. It's about all of that, sure. It is indeed another great coming-of-age tale that will satisfy fans of the genre, without a doubt. If you dug Robert McCammon's *Boy's Life* or Lansdale's *The Bottoms* or any of my own titles that I so shamelessly plugged above, you're gonna love Tamer Animals. If a beautifully-crafted coming-of-age tale is what you want, you're gonna get it. But, while I don't want to speak for Justin here, this one also feels like a love letter to the great horror flicks that were a part of the writer's own childhood. *Tamer Animals* isn't afraid to get gruesome once things start rockin' and rollin', and ultimately Justin's novel earns its place at the table among the twisted "family" of films and literature that many genre fans the same age as yours truly adored during their seminal years – flicks like the aforementioned *Chainsaw*, *Motel Hell*, and others of their era that adorned the covers of our beloved *Fangoria* magazines once upon a time. For yours truly, *Tamer Animals* brought to mind Jack Ketchum's classic novel *Off Season* as well, not to mention the work of Richard Laymon. I can't think of a better compliment to give a kick-ass writer who's only going to get more and more kick-ass as the years go by.

Justin Woodward's gonna be running with the big boys soon, if this keeps up.

You'll want to follow him wherever he takes you, I guarantee it.

Just be sure to watch out for what might be lurking in the woods . . . because the Goat Man, he's still out there.

James Newman
April 29, 2018

"Coheelee Creek Covered Bridge" by Tim Godwin

Artwork contributed by Gary Harbert

"We're all of us haunted and haunting."

\- Chuck Palahniuk

"Sometimes quiet is violent."

TWENTY ØNE PILØTS

STANTON

It's dangerous business walking out your front door. I've heard that said before, I'm sure of it, but I never quite understood how true it was until the summer of 2005. I find it hard to believe it's been twelve years already, but it has. Even though I'm a man of almost sixty now, there's a part of me that is only twelve years old. In a sense, a part of me was reborn that summer. I ain't talkin' about in a good Christian sense either. No, it ain't like that at all. I reckon there's just some things you can't witness and go on livin' the same way you did before. I know I couldn't.

Sometimes I wake up in the night and try to take off running across the house. No reason. Of course, I can't run. Can't walk hardly. On a couple of occasions, I actually hurt my wife, Kay. It was an accident each time, and she's since learned to get far away from me when I'm having one of my night fits. It being an accident don't make me feel any better about it though.

Most days I find it hard to find any kind of happiness. I'm not angry, not anymore. Defeated, maybe. I guess it's safe to say that I'm just not interested in sticking around this earth much longer. I turned on the TV the other day and I saw where this boy from Alabama set a tortoise on fire and filmed the whole thing. He put it on the internet. They say he was laughing while he did it. The worst part? There are thousands of people protesting because he got arrested. No one is held accountable anymore. I guess my point, if I had one, is that the world has gone to shit.

I got a letter the other day, and it said 'Dear Mr. Stanton, we want to have you on Good Morning

2 TAMER ANIMALS

America so we can talk to you about what happened and how it changed your life.' So, Kay says well, Paul, are you gonna do it? I told her I wasn't sure just yet. I said I didn't know what good it would do. Nobody wants to hear what I have to say.

CHAPTER ONE
Summer 2005
Dothan, Alabama

Patrick Hall rolled out of bed on the last day of his sophomore year of high school with a feeling of anticipation so strong he was almost sick with it. It hadn't been a bad year, but it hadn't been a great one either. It was the kind of year he could easily forget, like a movie that didn't quite leave enough of an impression for you to recall specific details a month later. The anticipation he felt wasn't so much for the last day of school as it was for what was coming after. He and his three best friends were planning a camping trip to Blakely, Georgia. They were going to stay at the campgrounds near the Coheelee Creek Covered Bridge. The only problem was that none of their parents would ever let them go if they really knew that was where they were going. The place had a reputation for being the place where people go when they want to do drugs and have sex, but Patrick and his friends were interested in the area for other reasons. Coheelee Creek was where you went if you wanted to see a ghost, and all the kids knew it.

Patrick shuffled across the room and stared into the mirror. His hair was a mop of brown, half-splattered to the side of his face. He contemplated whether he wanted to take a shower or not. Finally, he decided that he might as well get one. After brushing his teeth, he closed the bathroom door and pushed in the locking button. He removed his gym shorts and threw them into the hamper.

Staring into the mirror, he saw that he was gaining some weight. *Need to lay off the Doritos or you may never see your dick again*, he thought.

He turned on the water and ran his fingers under the stream, testing the temperature. Once it was comfortable, he slid into the shower. He stood there, swaying back and forth the slightest bit. His eyes threatened to close and he forced out a yawn; mornings weren't his specialty. He was startled when he heard knuckles rapping loudly on the bathroom door. His mom mumbled something about hurrying, that he had to take his little brother to school too. Sighing, he turned off the water and reached for a towel.

When he returned to his room, he checked his phone and saw that he had a text message from John Queen. He flipped open his phone and read the message: ***Still haven't got it, may need you to talk to Wolf for me***. He rolled his eyes. Wolf was the guy who could get it, but he was also the kind of guy who wanted you to enjoy it with him when you got it. Unfortunately for Patrick, he knew Wolf better than anyone else in their group. He debated on texting John back before finally sending back a single letter— ***K***.

John Queen was one of his best friends, and he was also coming on the camping trip. Aside from Patrick himself, John was the most organized person in their little group of friends. Most of the guys just went day to day without much thought on the future. They were the kind of guys who would go camping with nothing more than the clothes on their backs. People like that forced people like them—who actually prepared for things—to pick up the slack for them. They were always having to remind the others of everything they may not have thought of.

Patrick heard feet shuffling into his room. He looked over and saw his younger brother, Sam.

"I told you about dragging your feet," he said. Sam looked up at him and frowned. "I know," he said, breaking his gaze and staring at the floor.

"It's okay. It's just that middle school kids can be brutal. Don't want them having something to poke at you about, ya know?"

"Yeah."

The truth was that the sixth grade had been very hard on Sam, and Patrick knew it. He also knew that it didn't get any better; he had just gone through the same thing a few years back. He felt it was his responsibility and brotherly duty to give him a bit of a heads up—a crash course of sorts. It was only since starting middle school that Sam had developed the feet-dragging habit. It was as if his feet were too drunk to catch up with his legs. He did it without even realizing it; he would just shuffle around constantly, his feet dragging the ground like broken roller-skates. Their mother, Phyllis, had taken Sam for tests, afraid that it might be something wrong with him physically, but all the tests had come back negative. There were no muscle, bone, or nerve abnormalities, the doctor had said, no brain damage.

They were referred to a child psychologist named Doctor Roffsten, and against their father's many protests that Sam was just being a kid, Phyllis had scheduled an appointment.

On the day of the appointment, he had to drive Sam to the doctor's office, because it was scheduled just after school and their mother would be a few minutes late. He had planned to leave as soon as his mother arrived, but when she got there she told him that he needed to stay because she had to go back to work and he needed to take Sam home afterwards. So, he had been stuck staring at the aquarium in the waiting room and wondering if the bigger fish could eat the smaller one.

When they returned to the waiting room an hour and fifteen minutes (and a pile of money) later, his mother's face was all scrunched up as if in pain, tears silently streaked down the side of her cheeks. Sam was just following behind her, wide-eyed, as if he had just witnessed a monkey sing the Star-Spangled-Banner. She hadn't looked in his direction. She had just walked straight for the door, head lowered as if she were a ram. Pushing the door open, she went outside, both boys slowly following behind her.

Once they were outside, Phyllis hugged Sam and he climbed into his brother's car. As soon as the passenger door was closed, she turned on Patrick.

"Which... one... is Isaac Matthews? One of your friends?" She looked as if her spin on Wheel of Fortune had just landed her on the 'bankrupt' slot.

"What do you mean, which one?"

"I mean who the fuck is he?"

"He's a guy I know, he's younger than me though."

"But you're friends?" Her eyes twitched.

"No... I know his older brother alright, but not him. What's the deal?" He was getting frustrated. What could have happened in there to warrant him getting talked to like this?

"What's the deal, is that that sick little shit has been touching your brother!"

Patrick side-eyed the passenger seat of his car and saw that Sam had turned away from them and buried his face into his elbow.

"Seriously?" he asked. "Touching him... how?"

"I have to get back to work," she said, her voice wavering. "You need to talk to him, and you might want to warn your friend that his little brother will be hearing from the police." She reached for her car door and opened it, swinging her body inside and slamming the door shut. She rolled the window down about half-way and added, "That is, if your father hasn't already killed the fucker."

———※———

On the drive home, Patrick and Sam didn't speak. He dared a glance in his brother's direction at one point during the drive, saw Sam crying, and looked back at the road. What the hell do you say when you find out your little brother has been molested anyway? Sorry someone touched your thing, here's five dollars? It just wasn't something they could talk about, not yet.

They got home, and Sam said that he had a lot of homework to do and retreated to his room. Patrick walked into the kitchen and looked around. He wasn't sure what he wanted in there. Was it food? He eyed the counter where the cookies, chips, and sandwich bread sat. *No*, he thought, *I'm not hungry at all, not one bit*.

He walked over to where the counters made a right angle and knelt, opening the cabinet where his father stored the liquor. He began pulling out a dark bottle, and the glass clanked loudly against the other bottles. When he had it out of the cabinet, he stood up and turned the bottle over in his hands. The label read: JIM BEAM, and it was three-quarters full. Without thinking about it too long, he twisted the cap off and turned the bottle up, chugging the bitter stuff like a bum who had found a Gatorade in the street. He had never drunk alcohol in his life to that point, but he still wasn't dumb enough to think that this wasn't a terrible idea.

After he had chugged about a fifth of the remaining liquor, he slammed the bottle back onto the counter and spit into the sink. He half coughed, half sneezed and it felt like razors were crashing through his sinuses. He then washed the sink out, wiped the counter down, and twisted the top back on the bottle. He put the bottle back into the cabinet and scanned the area again to make sure he had cleaned it well enough. He figured his father would be furious if he knew what he had done. Something told him that his anger would be less about the underage drinking and annoying desperate teenage angst and more about how he was following in his footsteps.

He began walking towards the staircase to go to his room when his legs seemed not to want to move. Of course, he knew it was the alcohol making quick work of his teenage body, but the knowledge of that didn't stop him from staring down at his feet and chuckling dryly before uttering a short, distasteful comment to the empty room: "Oh, great... now someone's touched me too."

Phyllis called out again from the other side of the house that they were going to be late for school, and the boys looked at each other and smiled.

"She's such a spaz!" Sam said as he threw his hands into the air. They both laughed. Patrick thought he saw something in his brother's eyes behind the laugh though—a glint of pain.

"Come on," he said, clapping a hand on his brother's shoulder. "We'd better get going."

Sam's face flashed an awkward, sad kind of expression, one of admiration. He looked up to his older brother with such reverence, and he felt a little pathetic being so excited to have him touch his shoulder.

The two boys gathered their things and made their way into the kitchen. Their mother stood at the coffeemaker with her head down, her eyes closed.

"You okay, mom?" Patrick asked.

She looked in his direction, managing not to make eye contact. "I can't get this thing to work," she said. Her tone was an angry one.

He walked over to the coffeemaker, and she stepped out of his way. Lifting the lid, he pushed all the buttons. Nothing worked. He traced the cord out of the back of the machine and discovered that the coffeemaker was not plugged in. "Right here," he said. "We just forgot to plug it back in after we used the toaster is all."

"Thank you," she said, sounding defeated, pathetic. He gave her a sideways hug and said that they were leaving for school.

When they were in the car, Sam spoke up. "This is all my fault." He toyed with the zipper on his backpack.

Patrick thumbed through his CD case for something to pop into the player. He didn't like to ride in the car without music. "It is not," he said. Finally, he found the CD he was looking for: *My Chemical Romance: Three Cheers for Sweet Revenge*. He popped the disc into the player and looked over at his brother who was absentmindedly staring out of his window. The music blared much louder than he had intended and Gerard Way bellowed, "LONG AGO, JUST LIKE THE HEARSE YOU DIED TO GET IN AGAIN!!!"

He fumbled for the volume knob and turned the music down to a good calm level—a level a mother would approve of. He reversed the car out of the driveway and began the drive to the middle school. They probably were going to be late, but who gave a shit? It was the last day of school. Still, he didn't want Sam catching hell from an ambitious middle-school-teacher over something that wasn't his fault, so he drove with haste.

"What happened is not your fault," he reiterated. "And anyway, it's been six months. It's over."

"It is my fault though."

"How is it your fault, Sam? Did you ask for those boys to hold you down while Isaac Matthews groped you?" He hated himself already for saying it out loud.

Sam stirred in his seat. He opened his mouth and closed it again. Finally, he gathered the courage to say what he had wanted to say for so long.

"There's a reason they did that to me though, it wasn't just random," he said as he looked at Patrick. "You love me, right?"

"What?" He could feel his face heating up again as it reddened. Of course he loved his brother. It wasn't something that needed to be said. Was it?

"Never mind..."

"No... I do, Sam. Love you, that is." There was a long pause in which the awkwardness was so thick in the car, it almost oozed out of the cracked-open windows.

"Well then, hear me out," Sam was gathering his confidence. "I just can't have you laughing at me or judging me, it's why I haven't said anything yet. I know nobody will understand."

"I won't laugh," He was sure of this, he didn't feel like laughing at all. Puking, maybe, but not laughing.

"Well... do you remember when I used to spend the night over at Clark Hoover's house?"

"Yeah."

"Well this particular night, we were doing our usual thing, drinking cokes and playing Super Smash Brothers Melee on Clark's Gamecube, and then Isaac Matthews had just dropped in—you know I've never liked him—but him and Clark were friends and so I just dealt with it. But we were playing a tournament, and Clark's mom called out and said that Isaac was at the door, so she let him in. Anyway, he ended up staying the night, and he had brought these... porno movies over, and we watched them."

"That's all?" his brother let out a short bark of a laugh. "Every kid watches porn at some point or another, no biggie."

"No, that's not all," Sam said. "He put the movie in, and we were all watching, and then he just pulled out his penis in front of Clark and me. He told us to pull ours out too." His face was red, his voice shaking. He continued, "And then after Clark had fallen asleep, Isaac asked me to touch his penis, and I did. He asked me if I liked it, and I said that I did."

"Did you?" He didn't know what else to say; his heart was beating in his throat.

"I don't know. Maybe. Maybe I'm gay, I don't know. But then he told everyone that I was a fairy—a sissy. He humiliated me in front of everyone in the locker room."

"I think *he's* the sissy," Patrick said. They had arrived at the middle school now, and he had pulled the car into a parking space. "Listen, Sam," he said. "If you're gay... then who cares, you know? But don't let these fucking punks push you around, understand?"

"Yeah," Sam smiled. "But what if I'm not gay?"

"Makes no difference. You're just Sam, okay? You're my brother, that's who you are. Besides, you're only in the 6th grade, you've got a long time to figure out that kind of thing."

"About to be 7th grade," Sam said with a small smile as he got out of the car and shut the door.

Patrick arrived at school—late, of course—and pulled into the parking lot behind the building. The only spots that weren't already taken were the ones in the very far end next to the baseball diamond. He got out of his car, slid his cell phone under the driver's seat, locked the doors, and walked towards the building. As he walked, he admired the senior lot on the other side of the school, the one where even the furthest spot was still a hell of a lot closer to the building. Seniors got to decorate their spot at the beginning of the year. They also got out of class ten minutes before everyone else, so they could avoid the rush and leave earlier than the rest of the school. But he still had to make it through his junior year before he could join in that presidential bliss.

With his backpack slung over one shoulder—it was so heavy, but only nerds used both straps—he rounded the corner of the band building and made his way inside the main hall just as the tardy bell started to ring. *This is what Hell must feel like*, he thought. *Always late to something you didn't want to go to in the first place.*

The hallway was a total mess. It was as if the teachers had given up early this year. Posters hung askew on the walls, papers littered the floor, locker doors stood open at attention. Suddenly, a voice came flooding over the intercom system, babbling nonsense about making it a great day or not, the choice is yours.

He rounded the corner in the direction of his first class when he nearly bumped into Garrett Matthews. The two boys simultaneously made that *Ope* sound that people make when they're in someone's way. Upon realizing who it was that he had nearly collided with, his face flushed red. Garrett looked as if he wanted to cry, his lip quivered, his fist clenching and unclenching.

"I guess it's a good thing I didn't run into you," Garrett said. "I might have ended up in the hospital."

"Oh, go fuck yourself." he retorted. "Or maybe you wanna save that sexual tension for another guy."

Garrett let out a frustrated scream as his fist came crashing towards him so quickly that Patrick—although expecting it—still barely dodged it. The locker behind his head made a metallic slamming noise, and Garrett pulled his hand back, shaking it as if it was on fire. The sound of it echoed down the halls and caused the door closest to them to open. Coach Mathis, a history teacher, peered in their direction. He shielded his face from Garrett dramatically, as if he was in immediate danger of being hit. Coach Mathis looked at the locker behind his head.

"Now just what the hell are you doing, Matthews? It's like you don't want to play football next year!"

"But Coach, he—"

"Get in here," he said to Garrett, his voice firm. "And Hall, you get to class, hear?"

"Yes, sir."

Patrick walked away from the confrontation unscathed as Garrett was marched into Coach Mathis's room, probably for a referral to the principal. The whole thing between him and Garrett was incredibly awkward and totally out of their control.

It had happened like this: Patrick's father had come home from work on the day of Sam's appointment with Dr. Fishtank with one hell of a migraine. He got those sometimes. A lot of the time. He had taken a few swigs of Jim Beam (had the bottle seemed a little low?) and paced the kitchen saying he just didn't know what he was going to do, he just didn't know. Of course, Phyllis had told him what had happened to Sam, and Sam's insistence that it wasn't as bad as it seemed had only seemed to make him angrier. Phyllis tried to calm him, but somehow, she knew that would be fruitless. When Gary Hall decided to do something, it would not be stopped, especially not by his wife. Eventually, with a little help from Jim, Gary had gathered the courage to go and confront Isaac Matthews, a twelve-year-old boy. He insisted through slurred words that he was just going to talk, just talk. Phyllis had known better, but what could she have done? She considered calling the law on him herself, but ultimately, she decided against it. *Let him get himself in trouble*, she thought.

After some prodding, Gary had gotten Patrick to tell him where the Matthews' lived, and he had driven to their house and had knocked on the door continuously until someone had finally opened it, looking annoyed.

"Can I help you?" The man said.

"Are you Matthews?"

"My name is Rick Matthews, yes." His jaw seemed to dislocate, moving from side to side. "Who are you?"

"Your boy, Isaac. I need to see him now."

Rick could smell the sweet stink of liquor emanating from Gary. "What's this about?"

"I just need to... (hiccup) talk to your boy is all." He smiled a paper-thin smile.

"I'm afraid I can't let you do that, sir."

Gary stepped forward and put his hand on the door as if leaning on it for support. He moved as close to Rick as he could and whispered, "Why not?"

Rick's eyes flashed a nervous gleam, and he tried to shut the door, but Gary's hand was still holding it firmly open. "Honey, call the police," he shouted.

"What a great idea! I was thinking that same thing. You see, your boy—your faggot boy—has been messing with my boy, and I think the law would love to talk to him."

Rick hadn't waited to find out what Gary had been talking about. Taking the baseball bat which he had been clutching behind the door in his left hand, he pointed it at Gary's throat. "You get the fuck off my porch."

Gary threw his hands in the air and staggered backwards. "Okay, okay," he said. "I'm leaving." He half-turned on the porch before swinging back around grabbing onto the bat. It was too easy. He pulled Rick towards himself with the bat. All Rick had to do was let go of the bat, and Gary would have fallen flat on his drunk ass, but no, he held onto the bat. Gary pulled and pulled on the bat like a mime with an invisible rope. As soon as Rick was close to him, Gary had head-butted him, breaking his nose.

Soon after, he was hauled off to jail for that stunt, and everyone at the school knew it.

Patrick waited anxiously for the bell to ring after his first class. The school always held morning break after the first class of the day, and he needed to find John Queen and talk to him. He tapped his pencil on his desk like a nervous junkie as he stared at the clock. Kelsey Martin was side-eyeing him furiously.

"Will you stop that?" she whispered.

He stopped, his face turning a deep shade of red. Sighing, he placed the pencil down flat on the desk and crossed his hands in front of him.

Finally, the clock struck 9:15 and the bell rang for morning break. he found John outside by the snack machines. John was kneeling in front of the drink machine messing with the coin slot.

"What are you doing?" Patrick asked him.

John stood up quickly, a smile forming on his lips. "Nothing, what's up?"

"I need your share of the money."

"Have you got the other guys' money yet?"

"No, but I will." He knew what John was getting at. The other two guys were the ones he needed to be pestering about the money, not him.

They stepped aside as two girls approached to use the drink machine. They looked the girls up and down with their eyes once they had passed and then looked at each other. Their eyes were saying *Nice ass? Yeah. Nice ass.*

"Trust me, I'll get their money," Patrick insisted.

John pulled out his wallet and opened it, frowning. "Here's eight bucks," he said, handing him a crumpled five and three ones. "I'll have the rest in a minute."

The two girls at the drink machine started grumbling about something.

Patrick pocketed the money. "Where do you think Dean and Tim are?"

"I don't know. Didn't see them this morning at all. Probably hanging out in Betty, getting blazed."

There was a small tunnel two blocks away from the school which ran under the street. About six months prior, the guys were skipping school one day and discovered the tunnel. There was graffiti inside of it, but it was otherwise completely clean. The word BETTY was written on the side of the concrete tunnel in purple spray paint, so the guys just started calling the tunnel itself Betty. It was impossible to tell anyone was in there from the road, so it had become their hideout if they wanted to skip a class or two, or in the case of Dean and Tim, the whole day.

Some more kids were cursing the drink machine now.

"Well," he said. "They need to get their ass here soon. I'm going to Wolf's place after school."

"I know, I know. I'll text them and tell them to meet you at lunch."

The bell rang which told them that morning break was now over. John walked over to the drink machine and reached into the coin slot. He pulled out an orange handkerchief and cupped his hands below the slot. An avalanche of silver coins fell into his hands. He slipped the coins into the handkerchief and tied it loosely. Handing him the bundle of coins, John said "that should cover the rest of my share."

CHAPTER TWO

John Queen had always been what the adults would call a "straight shooter." He had always participated in extracurricular activities, was a member of the marching band, and was generally thought of as a good kid. As soon as he had turned sixteen years old, he had decided to get a job at the Winn-Dixie as a grocery bagger.

His plan was to work and save up the money to buy a car. His friend Patrick had been given a car by his parents on his sixteenth birthday. It was an old Ford Tempo, an ugly little thing, but it could take you places. John hadn't been so lucky. When John turned sixteen, his stepdad, Ronnie, handed him a twenty-dollar bill and told him not to spend it all in one place.

Saving up for a car had become increasingly difficult, though. Ronnie had developed the nasty habit of taking most of John's paycheck. Ronnie had taken John to get his check cashed one day after work; John didn't have a bank account yet, so Ronnie had processed it through his own. They went to the drive-thru at the bank, and he had John sign the back of the check. The teller processed the check and returned the cash in a small white envelope. Opening the envelope, Ronnie had counted the money, and taken out five of the twenties. He then had handed the crumpled envelope to John and driven away.

John had counted the remaining cash. $143.50. Looking at Ronnie with contempt, he said, "Why did you steal a hundred bucks from me?"

Ronnie had slammed the brakes on the car and pulled onto the side of the road. "What did you say to me? Stole?"

"Yes. You stole it. Why?"

"Let me ask you something," Ronnie began. "How much of that money would you have made if I hadn't given you the rides to and from work?"

"That's not—"

"And how would you have gotten the job in the first place if I hadn't driven you to the interview?"

"I—"

"Shut the fuck up."

Save for the occasional vehicle whizzing by, the car was silent. John had stared at Ronnie in fury. He had wanted to reach over to his side of the car and snatch the cash out of his pocket. If the truth was told, he had wanted to kill his stepdad—just fuck him up bad. Instead, he had turned away from him silently, clenched his fists and remembered what Ronnie had told him before, about how it would be a shame if John ever caused him to leave his mother. She wouldn't be financially stable without Ronnie. *I'd like to see how stable you'd be with no kneecaps,* he thought.

When they got home, John's mother had greeted them with as much enthusiasm as she could muster. John had stood in the doorway, tempted to speak out against Ronnie, to tell her what the bastard had done. He had opened his mouth to speak, but as soon as he had started talking, Ronnie had stepped on John's foot. *Hard.* John had cried out, and Ronnie had immediately begun apologizing. But as soon John's mother wasn't looking, Ronnie shot John a nasty look. *Tell her and see what happens.*

He never did tell her.

<hr>

After morning break had ended, John went to his second class of the day: Chemistry. He hated this class. Of course, they weren't doing any actual work today. The teachers who thought they were going to try that shit were going to be disappointed.

He sat down at his desk and pulled his phone out of his pocket half-way to see if either Dean or Tim had responded to him. Neither had. He double-checked to be sure the phone was on silent and shoved it back into his pocket.

The teacher, Mrs. Marcer, waddled into the room carrying her green bag, the same one she carried every day. No one had ever seen her open the bag. Not once had she needed anything out of there. The kids had begun to make jokes about it. "I heard it's all her dildos," Brad Eddins had said. "Yeah, they say she's terrified her husband will find them, all big and scary—black ones too. So, she brings them with her everywhere she goes." Another kid, Gordon Miller, had sworn that he had seen the bag move once.

She approached her podium and checked off the roll silently, her eyes flicking up and down from paper to seat. As she passed over Tim's seat, she looked back at her paper, back to the seat again, and then finally to John. John threw his hands up in the air, and she shook her head. John muttered something under his breath about fucking brother's keeper and luckily for him, Mrs. Marcer didn't hear him.

Mrs. Marcer addressed the room. "I know it's the last day of school, but—"

The entire class sighed. She went there.

"Listen," she continued. "Learning never waits." It was her trademark phrase. John imagined her bursting through a wall like the Kool-Aid man, her face all busted up and bleeding, teeth missing. But instead of saying "Oh Yeah!", she would shout "Learning never waits!" *Christ, what a moron.* Then John began to wonder what that glass is tempered with, the glass the Kool-Aid man was made of. That was some serious shit.

"Mr. Queen!"

Shit. He was doing it again. Living in his own world.

"Seven," he shouted. "The answer is seven." He was a snarky prick sometimes. The class laughed. Brad threw a wadded-up piece of paper at the back of John's head.

"Very funny, Mr. Queen," she said. "Let me know when they book you at the comedy club, I'll have to stop by and throw some quarters in a hat. You'll need them if your grades keep going the way they do."

Too much. That was too much and she knew it. He looked up at her with contempt as the class continued to laugh. Yes, yes, ladies and gentlemen, gather round and watch this grown woman who carries around a case of dildos—or severed heads—or whatever, pick apart a young man in a good, old-fashioned roast. Hilarious. He slunk into his seat and stared at the clock until it was time to leave.

The truth was that John's grades had suffered. Anyone with any insight into his home life would find the cause without much trouble. He was working all the time he wasn't at school. It had even gotten necessary for him to ask his boss for more hours, taking up his entire weekend—*each weekend*—as well as school nights. Ronnie had gotten even more greedy now, taking from every paycheck that John had earned.

John had finally decided that he had to let his mom know what he had been doing. He had been warned, of course, that Ronnie could and would leave her if John caused him any trouble, but John had decided that it didn't matter much anymore. If Ronnie was treating John like this, then how was he treating his mother? Another point of contention he had decided on was the matter of his paychecks. If Ronnie left them, John could offer to help pay the bills. His money had already been taken from him against his will, he would much rather offer it willingly if it meant that Ronnie would take a fucking hike. *Just let me get through this trip*, was the thought that kept circling in John's head. They had been planning this trip for so long, and he didn't want this messing it up.

CHAPTER THREE

Dean Fredrick was not having the best morning. Before he even woke, he was having one of his nightmares. Nightmares were a regular thing for Dean, but this one was a real son-of-a-bitch. This time, however, it was entirely his own fault. The night before, in anticipation of the upcoming trip, he had done some research on the Coheelee Creek Covered Bridge. He and the other guys had heard about ghost sightings. That was cool, but he didn't know if he really believed them. It was easy to dismiss ghost sightings. But what he had seen on his computer screen was real.

There were two things in particular which had bothered Dean the most. At the top of the page was an article about The Hanging Tree. Not even a mile from where they would be camping, there was a tree where the local law enforcement was said to have hanged vile criminals a century ago. There was a picture next to the article of a noose tied to a low-hanging branch. The local Sherriff, Paul Stanton, had made a comment on the matter: "Yes, we know of the hanging tree, but it's just a myth. Something kids like to talk to pass the time." When asked about the noose reappearing, he said, "I admit that I have cut the noose down myself several times, only to find it back the next day. But like I said, practical jokers, bored kids. Maybe one day I'll bring my trail-cam down there and we'll have a face."

It was obvious that the writer of the article was a little biased, but it didn't matter to Dean. He believed every word of it. But the second occurrence from the area scared him even more. There was a single word at the beginning of the article: GOATMAN. Not goat man, or even goat-man.

GOATMAN.

The article had told the story of a black goat farmer that had moved his family into the area in the 1930s and found success and some local popularity. The Klansmen and local government were upset by this and sought to destroy him. One night, the Klansmen had found "The Goatman" and attacked him viciously, finally dragging him to The Hanging Tree and brutally hanging him from the noose which hung there.

The story said that when the Klansmen had finished the job, they turned to leave, only to hear a small noise from behind them—a small bleat like that of a distressed goat. When they had turned around, they found that the body of the Goatman had vanished.

There was only a lonely hanging noose.

In anger and fear, the Klansmen were said to have gone back to the residence of the Goatman and murdered his wife and two small children in cold blood. The kicker of the story—the thing that got Dean's heart really racing—was that they say the Goatman's body had never been found, and that as recently as the early 2000's, there had been numerous sightings of a strange man walking through the woods of southwest Georgia.

A local musician, Willie Fred McPhree, had been quoted as saying, "I've seen the Goatman twice. Both times, he was down on all fours, just off the road. He was wearing furs or pelts or something. The worst part, though, is that it looked like he had hooves... and horns." The local man had gone on to say that he had nearly crashed his car both times because he hadn't been able to look away from the Goatman. A chill had crawled up Dean's spine at the last bit. Couldn't look away. As freaked out as Dean was, he was ecstatic to tell his friends what he had read. He also wanted to find out if anyone had a gun they could take with them. Just in case.

Dean checked the time in the bottom corner of his computer: 11:45 PM. It was late, and he had school the next day. He closed the laptop and stood up, suddenly realizing that he was in total darkness. This awareness normally would not have bothered him, but under these circumstances...

The hallway was fifteen miles long, the floor was a mess of gnashing teeth and gums, the walls perspired blood. Dean was also pretty sure there was a dead man behind his open bedroom door, but he had to piss. Badly. He gathered all his courage and scrambled across the room to the lamp in the corner, flicking it on. Okay, so there was no actual danger in his room that he could see. Still, he didn't want to chance the hallway. He found an empty bottle in his trash can, pissed in it, and shoved it down to the bottom of the trash. He climbed into bed, leaving the light on and the door open, and drifted off to an uneasy sleep.

***

The woods were cold and dark. He made his way through them with great unease, his feet seeming to float rather than making contact with the ground as he stepped along. A thick fog in the air made it difficult to see much more than a few feet ahead or behind him. A loud crash behind him startled him, and he jumped, his heart leaping into his throat. A figure strode past him making gurgling noises, but Dean couldn't make out what it was; he backed up against a tree as he heard feet stamping by. When it got closer, he saw what it was: a black goat running past him. Only this goat didn't have a head. The neck of the goat was cut off in a messy stump, black blood spurting from the hole. Dean tried to scream but was unable to make any sound. The goat turned as if looking at him when it passed by, and it went on walking for a few yards before crashing down on the ground and convulsing sickly.

Dean felt something move against his back, which was firmly planted against a tree. The writhing, wriggling thing on his back caused him to jump forward and wheel around. Snakes crawled all over the tree, crisscrossing each other in an orgy of bodies, each of them ivory-scaled with shining, hateful red eyes.

Then, out of the corner of his eye, Dean saw a little girl approaching him.

She was singing and Dean saw that she had a small rusty hatchet in her hands. He started to say something to her when he heard a second little girl singing from another direction.

Suddenly, Dean realized that both girls were pointing above his head. He looked up and saw that he was standing under a rope—a noose. Horror struck him as he turned to run, but he couldn't move. His feet seemed glued to the ground. The girls approached, and he clawed at them in vain. They raised their hatchets in unison and struck.

Dean woke with a start and glanced at the clock next to his bed.

6:58.

Fantastic, he thought. His alarm was set for 7:00.

His arms were pickled ripe with gooseflesh. As he sat up in the bed, he felt the coldness below him; he had been sweating heavily. There was no noise coming from downstairs, no clinking of plates, no TV running, no people talking. Dean's parents were divorced, and his mother had won custody of him. His dad wasn't a bad guy; he just wasn't his mother. The courts usually went with the mother.

Dean's mom worked early shifts at the Waffle House, so Dean had to be self-reliant in getting to school on time. Or at all. But she did her best to take her breaks in time to call and make sure he had woken up and was getting ready for school. Not that he couldn't lie, but she did the best she could.

In general, Dean had done well taking care of himself. He didn't have a car, but he usually caught rides with another kid who lived a street over, Christopher Lucas. He and Chris weren't good friends, but they got along well enough to ride to school together. If Chris wasn't going to school, there was always the bus.

Dean stood up and walked slowly to his closet. He opened the door and immediately screamed, jumping backwards. Hanging in the closet, between his plaid shirts and his hoodies, was a noose. But of course, it wasn't actually there.

Was it?

He looked again and saw just the most ordinary closet one could hope for.

———————◇◇———————

After Dean's second class of the day—Anatomy and Physiology—he walked out into the hallway and saw John leaving his Chemistry class, looking flustered.

Dean called, "Hey John!"

John turned around and saw Dean waving his arms anxiously. He looked like a rabid Iron Maiden fan calling out to Bruce Dickinson from behind a ticket line.

John walked over to Dean and said, "What's up? Have you seen Tim yet?"

"No," Dean said. "I was thinking we should probably go look for him, ya know, in his spot."

John laughed. "Yeah," he said. "But it's the last day. I don't understand why he wouldn't come hang out with us a little."

Dean and John walked out of the building and made their way over to the band building, the least conspicuous way to leave the school without being stopped by a nosy teacher.

As they passed by the doors to the band building, John said, "I've got to take a piss real quick. You?"

"Nah," Dean said. "I'll wait out here."

John opened the doors and disappeared into the band building. Dean walked over to the outside water fountain and had a drink. He had to press down hard on the rusty metallic button for a small stream to come out. He stuck his face down in a sort of submission to the water fountain—to his human need of hydration—and began to lap up the coppery tasting lukewarm water.

"Hey Fredrick! Fuck you doing, boy?" A voice called out from behind him.

Dean turned around and saw a gang of four guys standing, arms crossed, staring at him. The furthest on the left—the one who had spoken—was Jamal Jenkins, Dean's cousin on his father's side. He and Jamal were friends when they were younger, before high school, before middle school even. As far as Dean could tell, Jamal's biggest problem with Dean was his choice of friends, or more importantly, their race. It was an ugly thing, really. The thing was, Dean was mixed, half Japanese and half black. This had earned him the distasteful slur of Blackanese from some people—some friends, some not. It didn't really bother him being called Blackanese. He actually found it quite funny, if not a bit lame. It was too easy.

"Nothing," Dean said, eyeing the group.

Jamal rolled his eyes. He wanted Dean to say something out of line. He wanted a confrontation.

Unfortunately for Jamal, Dean was in no mood for that, and he was willing to stay as neutral as possible in hopes that Jamal would get bored and shove off.

John walked out of the band building wiping his hands on his jeans. "Dude, they're still playing in there it's so—" he stopped as he saw the group of black kids cornering Dean. "What's up?" he said to the small crowd.

"What's up! What's up?" Jamal raised his voice. "You trying to fight?"

John had seen this before. Jamal had a way of pissing off the Pope. Deciding not to let it work on him, he said simply, "Come on man, let's go." He was looking at Dean.

Dean started walking towards John.

"That's right," Jamal said. "Be a good nigga and obey your mastah." The boys sniggered and jeered.

John said, "He's not—"

"Why are you guys laughing?" Dean interrupted, gesturing towards Jamal's friends. "You do everything Jamal says, when he says it. Seems to me you guys are the ones with a master."

One of them spoke up, a boy named Demetrius Smith. "Least we ain't hanging around with no fuckin honkey."

John's face turned red.

Dean clenched his fists and stepped towards the group.

"Come on, Dean," John said. "They're not worth it."

"Come on Dean, they're not worth it." Jamal said in a whiny voice. "Ain't nobody talkin' to you, boy."

"I ain't done nothin' to you," John retorted. "None of you. So just screw off."

Jamal said, "I thought you'd be a little smarter, Dean, all that Jap in you. But I guess I was wrong. Let me know if you ever decide to drop your dipshit friends." And he turned and walked away.

His posse followed him.

Dean considered following after them, calling out an insult or a retort, but he didn't. He looked at John instead. "Hey man... I—"

"Don't worry about it," John said. "Let's just go find Tim."

———◦———

They headed west on Selma Street, being careful not to look suspicious. Once they had cleared school property, John spoke up.

"I just don't get it, man."

"What?" Dean said, but he knew what.

"Why is race such a big deal to them?"

Dean shrugged. "Why is it such a big deal to anyone?"

"It's not to me."

"John, it's Dothan, Alabama. It's at least somewhat of a deal to everyone. Hell, forget Dothan. It's a deal everywhere. You know it's true."

John looked puzzled.

"Everyone is a little bit racist," Dean continued. "It's human nature, man. It's the same reason cats hiss at dogs: they're not their kind. It's the same reason birds don't hang out with fish."

"Okay," John said. "Just a couple problems with what you said."

"Yeah?"

"Yeah. First of all, some cats hiss at other cats too. Also, you're talking about different species there. Humans are humans. We're all the same."

"Are we though?"

They rounded a curve and turned left onto the street where Betty was.

John said, "Yeah, for the most part."

"Look," Dean said. "All I'm saying is people feel comfortable around their own race, in general. I'm not saying Jamal is right though—he's a prick—I'm just explaining it to you. You know I don't fall into the same line of thought. If I cared what anyone thought, I wouldn't hang out with three incredibly white guys all the time, would I?" He laughed.

"Watch it," John said, smiling. "You racist." He punched Dean on the shoulder.

"You're the racist!" Dean yelled in an over-the-top manner, waving his hands, and they both collapsed into laughter.

"Yeah. You know what, all you fuckin' Blackanese people are the same. Just a bunch of fools, I tell ya! Don't know whether to steal a car or not cause they sure as hell can't drive it."

"And you whiteys with your nice houses and your credit cards and your 401k's. The worst."

They breached the hill in the middle of the street and saw police lights flashing. There was a police car parked on the side of the road where the bridge was. Where Betty was.

CHAPTER FOUR

Tim Johnson woke on the last day of his sophomore year of high school with an erection. A real proud one.

A triumphant exclamation point to the sky.

Good morning, America.

This was not unusual for any hormonal teenager. But for Tim, it was nearly constant, and not just good ole' morning wood either. All kinds of boners, for all kinds of reasons, and the occasional for no reason at all.

But more on that later.

For now, there was the problem, or not-problem to deal with, and boy did he like dealing with it.

He rolled out of bed and reached into his dresser-drawer and pulled out a Ziploc bag and a small bottle of Jergens Ultra-Healing lotion. He turned on his TV and turned up the volume. Patrick Star was fucking up some simple task in an epic way.

There was no need to lock the door, it was already locked. His mother preferred it that way.

But more on that later.

Tim turned the Ziploc bag inside-out and squirted the perfect amount of Jergens into the turned-out portion of the bag. Kneeling, he placed the bag between the mattress and the box-spring so that only the end stuck out of the side.

When Tim entered his kitchen before leaving for school, he saw his father standing on the other side of the room reading the newspaper with his back turned towards him.

"Morning, Tim."

"Hey, Dad."

Tim reached into the pantry and grabbed the box of chocolate Pop-Tarts.

Still not looking in Tim's direction, Wendell Johnson asked, "You got a girlfriend yet, Tim?"

Tim was working on getting the silvery plastic off his Pop-Tart, but his hands stopped working for a moment. Without looking up he said, "No."

Wendell turned his head, sighing quietly. "But you'd like one?" He said.

"Sure, I guess." Tim blushed, still looking down. This conversation happened way too often.

"I just mean to say...well, I just want you to be smart is all. And careful."

Ah yes, thought Tim.

Careful.

Of course.

The girls were just lining up for him.

"Yeah, Dad. You don't have to worry," is all he said.

But Wendell did worry. Wendell worried a lot.

And for good reason, really.

Tim had been diagnosed as having extremely high levels of testosterone, enough to place him into the category of 'Teen Sex-Addict' by some doctors. This title seemed ridiculous for someone whose only crime was that he had developed early. And strongly.

His family had become concerned when Tim had come to them with a question about some hair he was growing—pubic hair, specifically—when he was only seven years old.

Precocious puberty, the doctors had called it, and it was extremely rare. For Tim, it meant that he had very high testosterone, levels higher than a grown man.

This meant that if your average teenager thought about sex every fifteen seconds, Tim thought about sex every three seconds. Everyday items caused Tim to get an erection.

Milk: jugs.

Grass: pubic hair.

Flagpole: you know.

Luckily for Tim, he had managed (for the most part) to control his problem and mask it enough so he could maintain friendships.

In other words: his friends didn't know he was a freak.

But there was the one thing...

Three months ago, when it was still cold outside, Tim had been walking out of the lunchroom when he spotted something out of the corner of his eye.

Kelsey Martin (Patrick had a crush on her and everyone knew it) was bending over to fix her flip-flop. And normally, it being cold and all, Kelsey would be wearing some modest and conservative clothing, but on this particular day, she had decided to wear a sundress, of all things. She had a denim jacket over the dress, her arms inside the jacket rather than inside the sleeves of the jacket.

What Tim saw when he looked in her direction was that it was very windy that day, and from the angle where he stood, there was something showing out of the top of her dress.

Kelsey Martin had opted out on a bra this day, and Tim could see not only her entire breasts, but her nipples.

Hot damn.

Now, if this particular score had been discovered by any other boy in the school, it would have been pretty hard not to get worked up over. But for Tim Johnson, well...

Tim lurched forward a few steps and dropped to his knees. He uttered a ridiculous choked sound. People stared. One girl asked if he was okay.

The thing was, he normally wore tight, restricting jeans which helped with his problem more often than not, but today, much like Kelsey Martin, Tim had made an ill-advised wardrobe choice. He had gone with sweatpants.

His penis jumped away from his body like a man jumping off the sinking Titanic. That is to say it was utterly pathetic and sad. And where was the goddamn bathroom anyways?

By now there was quite a crowd, and he couldn't just sit there on his knees like a lazy baseball catcher forever, could he? He decided to get up and use his bookbag to shield his front, maybe someone would think he had thrown up on himself.

No matter what, he had to get out of there. He ran down the hallway and managed not to run into anyone. Most of the teachers and students were outside or in the lunchroom.

He made it to the bathroom and quickly entered a stall, pushing it closed behind him. He went to lock the latch, but he noticed that the lock was broken.

Too late.

He backed up a step and dropped his pants and began to masturbate frantically. It was as if he was playing the most intense game of Yahtzee you could imagine.

His mind played images over and over of Kelsey Martin and her pink nipples. He wasn't proud of this...need. He hated his body and his mind for what it did to him, but he couldn't worry about that now. Because right now he was climbing the mountain, and he was reaching the peak and as the Bible says, he saw that it was good.

Now we come to the important part of this story, the part that changed things for Tim Johnson. The thing was, in his delirium and mad-dash to the bathroom, he had entered the girls' room rather than the boys'. If he had just looked around at all, he may have seen that the bathroom had no urinals, or the fact that there were little receptacles for feminine products, but the truth was that he didn't have his eyes open much at all. He had them closed, and he was playing back some recent footage in his mind.

Back to the peak.

The peak was good. So good, in fact, that he didn't hear the stall door opening when a freshman named Erica Kline opened it and saw the peak for her own eyes. She just stood there staring like Carol Anne stared at her TV in *Poltergeist* — terrified and unable to move.

What happened next was that Tim Johnson had to go to a lot of sit-down-meetings with his parents and some teachers, and eventually, doctors of the mental nature. Tim's parents were handed pamphlets of information about sex criminals and legal implications.

Tim had overheard some of the conversations he wasn't supposed to hear between his parents as well. Some key phrases were thrown around. But his least favorite of them all was future rapist.

No son of mine, Wendell Johnson had said.

Tim felt alone. He wanted to tell them so many things. Like how he had just fucked up and went into the wrong bathroom, but he knew that had little to do with the core concerns they had. Erica Kline had just been the catalyst to cause it all to come to light. They knew that he had been a frequent masturbator, there was no hiding it when you lived with him. Which brings us to the reason why Tim's mother didn't mind if he kept his door locked.

It's simple really: they show butts on TV.

On cable.

Tim had turned on his TV for background noise while he played *World of Warcraft* with his friends online, and there was Halle Berry's ass on his screen in high definition.

His mother had knocked on his door five minutes later and said that dinner was ready.

He said, "I'm coming."

Aggravated, she had entered the room anyway and found he wasn't lying.

⸻◦⸻

Now, Tim considered himself lucky. Erica Kline had not told any students what she had seen. It had been requested heavily by the counselors who assured her that it was being taken care of, and student chatter would have made things worse for her.

They were right, really. High-schoolers could be terrible towards each other. It was in her best interest just to push it out of her mind as if it had never happened. She was, however, promised that she would not have to take any classes with Tim Johnson ever again, they would make sure that scheduling mess would never occur. And of course, Tim did his best job to avoid her, but they still occasionally passed in the halls in awkward avoidance.

⸻◦⸻

Wendell Johnson waved goodbye to his son that morning and watched him get on the bus for school. If the truth were told, he was relieved.

Tim arrived at school before any of his friends. He walked around, waiting for the bell to signal the start of his first class. He spotted Erica Kline across the soccer field and turned to go the other way.

Why does my bus have to be so early?

In haste, he made his way to the playground next to the school. Tim crossed the small bridge between the properties and sat down on one of the swings. Swinging forward slowly, his mind wandered.

Don't get horny, he thought.

He thought of sports. Baseball, specifically. The Braves. He imagined Chipper Jones crushing a grand slam out of Turner Field; Tim Hudson pitching a no-hitter against the good-for-nothing Mets. He imagined girls in the stands jumping up and down, titties bouncing.

Fuck.

Okay, something else.

Of Mice and Men, the book Tim's English class had just finished. It was weird, wasn't it? Yes. That damned retard guy didn't know when to quit, did he? Tim suddenly wished that someone would put him out of his misery like an old dog with no teeth.

A noise came from his left.

Tim glanced around the playground searching for the source of the noise. After looking around for a moment, he decided it must have just been in his mind. He turned and walked towards the school.

The noise again.

Tim turned and stared behind him. He walked slowly towards the large plastic tubes on the playground. Walking up the steps, Tim heard the noise again, it sounded like... a moan.

He bent over and peered into the plastic red tube and saw two Senior girls whose names he didn't know. One of them had her face between the other's legs.

"Oh shit!" he said, stupidly.

The girl who was doing the work turned and saw him. "Oh my God, get out of here you creep!"

Tim ran away, laughing. The bulge in his pants throbbed. He turned and ran down the street in the direction of Betty the tunnel. He had something to take care of.

———————⊰◈⊱———————

Tim turned right at the dead end and nearly ran into someone. Elmer Davis, a black boy in their grade, was standing on the street corner, eyes wide.

They stared at each other.

"Don't go," said Elmer.

How could he know where I'm going, thought Tim. *Has he been following me? Has he been watching me?*

"I don't know what you're talking about."

Elmer continued to stare. His body started shaking, his eyes rolled in his head.

"Holy shit, dude! Are you having a seizure?"

Elmer made choking sounds and fell to the ground and started flopping. Tim started shouting for help. A woman came out of her house across the street and ran over to them.

"Call 9-1-1 please," Tim said.

Reaching her shaking hand into her back pocket to grab her cell phone, she asked, "What happened?"

"I think he's having a seizure," said Tim.

"Grab his tongue or something!" The woman shouted. Her voice was shaky. Tim couldn't help but notice that she was very attractive. She couldn't have been older than twenty-five.

"I can't just stick my hand in his mouth," Tim said. "He'll bite my fingers off!" He pulled out his wallet and shoved it into Elmer's mouth.

The woman was talking with an emergency dispatcher.

"Yes, that's right. I run Lots of Tots daycare. My name is Wendy. Yes. Well, it's my house. Yes, right down from Dothan High School. Okay, thank you."

Tim and Wendy stood together and waited for the ambulance to arrive. Elmer had gone stiff, but his eyes were still moving frantically, and his nose was bleeding. Tim wondered if Elmer was going to die. That would be strange, to see someone die like this, or at all really. But then, of course, he would be able to tell people, "I watched a guy die once." People would be standing around at their fancy office party exchanging stories about their kids in little league and Tim would have the option—should he choose to utilize it—to just walk up and tell everyone he watched a kid die.

Still, he didn't want it to happen. Elmer had always been nice to Tim the few times they had interacted.

The ambulance arrived at nearly the same time as the police. Two EMT's got out of the vehicle and trotted over to where Elmer lay on the ground.

"Whose is this?" one of them said, holding a spit-covered wallet in the air.

"That's mine," said Tim, grimacing.

"That's good thinking, son."

Tim nodded and watched the men work. Elmer was mumbling something that sounded like 'ridge'.

A police officer approached Tim and Wendy and asked for their stories. Tim talked nervously, explaining what he could about the situation, and Wendy interjected where she felt necessary.

After the officer thanked Wendy, she turned and went back into her house. Tim turned to walk back in the direction of the school.

"Where you headed son?"

"Oh," said Tim, "I was just gonna go on to school now."

"It's two blocks away," the cop said. "I'll take ya, hop in." He gestured to the back seat of the cruiser. "Besides, you're late now. I can explain to the school what happened."

Tim didn't care what the school thought.

"Thank you," he said.

The cop smiled. "It's no problem."

Tim hopped in the back of the car.

The officer climbed into the driver's seat and turned, looking at Tim as if to check that he was still there. He picked up his radio. Tim shifted uncomfortably, realizing he was sitting where the rapists and murderers sit.

"This is Officer Yates. I need a representative from CPS to head to Dothan High School, estimated time eleven-hundred. Better have someone from juvie too." He hung the mic back on its clip.

"What was that?" Tim said. "CPS? You mean like, child protective services?"

"That's correct." Officer Yates was writing something on a clipboard.

Tim felt for the handle of the car and pulled gently.

"You know that won't work," Yates said without even turning his head. And then he turned on the siren and drove down the street, passing over the tunnel and turning right in the direction of the school.

Tim saw John and Dean staring at him—jaws open—as the car flew past them.

CHAPTER FIVE

Patrick snuck out to his car to check his phone, cursing himself for not just keeping it on him. The problem was that the school had gotten so strict about the dumbest shit, and all students were subject to search at any time. He had been unlucky once and received three days of in-school-suspension for having his cell phone.

He knew he had limited time since his teacher, Mr. Robertson, had only really excused him to use the bathroom. He sprinted down the hallway, making sure no one saw him and bolted outside.

When he made it to his car, he heard his phone ringing before he even unlocked the door. He fumbled with the keys and dropped them to the ground, sighing. And then he heard the siren.

Looking down the street, he saw the police car headed in his direction.

Damn it, he thought. *I just wanted to check my phone. That's all.*

Patrick knelt quickly between his car and a green Jeep that was parked next to his car, grabbing his keys and staring through the windows. The police cruiser passed by the parking lot, and there was someone in the back seat. The car was slowing down, turn signal flashing.

He opened the door and snatched his cellphone from under the seat.

John was calling.

"Hello?" said Patrick.

Panting and obviously out of breath, his friend said, "They've... got... Tim!"

He looked up from his phone and saw Dean and John running down the street in the direction of the police car, John had his phone to his ear. He closed his phone and ran over to them.

John was still talking into his phone when he reached them. "Whoa, where the hell did you come from?"

"Never mind that. What's going on?

Officer Yates parked the car in front of the school, there were a few kids walking outside. A few teachers, surprised by the flashing lights, came outside to see what was going on.

Tim could feel his heart attempting a jailbreak, but the bars of his ribcage were too strong. A cold sweat had begun to form on his forehead. He looked out the window and saw his three friends gathered by a far wall, their mouths open.

"You gonna come in quietly, or do I need the cuffs?" Yates asked him.

Tim said nothing.

"Quietly, it seems." He laughed.

Officer Yates opened his door and got out of the car. He walked around to Tim's side of the car and opened his door.

"Stand up."

Tim stood up.

Officer Yates put his hand on Tim's shoulder and led him inside the school.

"Did he kill somebody?" Patrick asked.

"How should we know?" Dean said with the slightest hint of a smile on his lips.

"Course he didn't kill no one," said John.

"Well then, what happened?"

"Me and John went to go check on Tim, since no one had heard from him, you know?" said Dean. "And we figured he was probably hanging out in Betty, so we walked down there."

"And the cop was putting Tim in the car when we got there," John finished.

"So then, how do you know he didn't kill anyone?"

"What the hell are you talking about?" asked Dean.

Patrick held up his hands in frustration. "I don't know, maybe he was sitting in the tunnel playing his PSP, and a fucking hobo showed up and tried to take it from him, and he stabbed him in the eye with a pencil."

John and Dean exchanged glances and burst out in laughter almost simultaneously.

He stared at them amusedly. "I'm just saying," he said.

"First of all," John said, "if he murdered someone in that tunnel, there would be all kinds of people there. Ambulances, firetrucks, the national fucking hobo society—"

Dean laughed loudly.

John continued, "And they wouldn't be taking Tim back to school, they'd be taking him to jail, man."

"It's not like I was totally serious."

Tim sat down in a chair in the Principal's office. He stared down at his fingernails. The police officer was talking to Principal Harris in the next room.

What were his parents going to say?

Was Elmer okay?

What was his crime here, really?

Suddenly, Officer Yates came out of the office and sat down next to Tim. He smelled like a mixture of pine needles and Febreze.

"Listen, son. I hope I haven't scared you too much. But you need to understand something. When I was your age, I used to dick around like you all the time. I didn't take school seriously, took me a long time after the real world hit me for me to get my shit together. And it pisses me off to see kids skipping school and fuckin' off—sorry—like you've been doing. I used to go to this very school, and I know it sucks. Don't tell anyone I said that, but you need to be in school, man. I've worked this area for a while now, and I've seen you walking up and down the streets during school hours. It was time you learned your lesson."

Officer Yates stood up. "Hold out your arms."

Tim reluctantly held his arms in front of him like a sleepwalking bear. Officer Yates pulled his nightstick from its holster and drew back.

Tim winced.

Quickly and as gentle as a butterfly landing, he popped Tim on the wrist.

"Now go in there, Principal Harris needs to talk to you." He turned to walk out of the room. Turning, he said, "Stay out of trouble, Mr. Johnson."

Tim knocked on Principal Harris' door.

"Come in." Came the voice from the other side.

Tim opened the door, and Principal Harris reached out his hand as if he wanted Tim to shake it.

Awkwardly, Tim reached his hand out, a bit apprehensive.

"I just wanted to shake your hand, son," said the principal. "Officer Yates tells me your quick thinking and action possibly saved another student's life this morning."

Tim was astounded.

Harris continued, "And while I have no idea what both of you were doing off school property when it happened, Officer Yates assured me that it was definitely before school began this morning. Is that correct?"

"Y-yes sir." Tim stammered.

"Fantastic. No harm done then." Principal Harris was thinking of how good of a reflection this was on the school. A white student uses quick thinking to save the life of a fellow black student using knowledge he gained while attending his school. The implications. "Tell you what, Tim. It's the last day of school, how about you take the rest of the day, and start that summer vacation early. You've earned it."

Tim was still in shocked disbelief.

"Yes, sir," he said finally. "Sounds great."

"Have you got a way home?"

"Yes, sir."

"Great." This was a good thing. He didn't need Tim telling the whole school what happened.

Tim walked out of the front doors of his school early that day, unsure whether he should feel pride or some other feeling. He stood, hands on hips, shirt flapping in the wind, and gazed around the campus wondering how he was really going to get home. He had lied to Principal Harris, of course; he didn't have a car.

"Hey, Charles Manson, they really let you out already?" John said from Tim's left.

Tim turned and saw the three of them watching him. His face flushed. He dropped his hands from his hips quickly.

Tim told the three of them what happened, leaving out, of course, his motive for wanting to go to the tunnel. Instead, he said he had put an SNES emulator on his PSP, and he had planned on trying to beat Super Mario World this morning. The group of them listened intently, only speaking when they were sure he was done talking.

"Hot shit, man," Patrick said. "That's awesome."

"Does your wallet have teeth marks on it?" Dean asked.

"If it does, it's from you getting too close when you kiss his ass," John said, making kissing noises.

They all laughed.

"Only problem is I told him I had a way home," said Tim.

"You do," said John. "Right Pat?" He looked in the direction of the back parking lot. Towards Patrick's car.

Patrick thought for a moment. He looked at Dean. "You cool with this, too?"

"Yeah man, fuck it, let's go." Dean said.

"Okay. Fuck it."

CHAPTER SIX

The four of them walked to Patrick's car as he unlocked the doors. John called shotgun and climbed in the front seat. Dean and Tim each took a seat in the back and shoved the random trash out of their way. Patrick reached for a flyer that was stuck under his windshield wiper and read it aloud: "My Last Midnight and Little Girl Lost. End of school bash. Five bucks to get in."

He tossed the flyer onto the center console, and Dean reached for it and read it for himself. "No way I'm going," he said.

"Oh my God," said Tim. "Is this about Paige Jackson? Let her go, dude."

Paige Jackson was Dean's ex-girlfriend. She had dumped Dean at a My Last Midnight show at the old Wired venue.

But the way that she had broken up with him was the worst. She had begged Dean to take her to the show all week, so he had gotten Patrick to sort of chauffeur them around for the night, an excuse to include him on the show too, since he had also wanted to go.

The two of them had picked up Paige and taken her to eat at TGI Fridays. After dinner, they had gone to Wired—the local coffee shop which also hosted bands—for the show.

During the night, Paige had been acting strange towards Dean. And when the band started playing, she got up and started dancing obnoxiously in front of the lead singer. The singer took off his shirt and threw it on the ground, growling into the microphone and climbing the wooden ceiling supports like King Kong. He seemed to sing every word to Paige.

My Last Midnight was known for their antics, but this still bothered Dean. What the hell was this guy trying here? Suddenly, Paige trotted over to where Dean and Patrick were standing. The band was between songs and the singer announced that the next song was a slow one called Coloring Book.

"Oh my God, I love this one!" Paige exclaimed to Dean.

Dean said, "That's great." His frustration was visible.

"Look," she said. "I can't do this anymore. I've been meaning to give this to you." She looked at Patrick as she shoved a note into Dean's hand. "Thanks for the ride," she said. She turned and ran back to the front of the crowd.

Dean looked down at the folded note in his hands. He opened it and read the note:

Everyone's been telling me that you are social suicide. And I can't cope with these feelings that you're giving me. I wanted you to want me for me, but now all you want is my body. I really hate to leave you on a night like this.

Paige

She had broken up with him for the singer from My Last Midnight. What was worse, she had done it using their lyrics.

Patrick pulled the car over to the side of the road. "Where am I going?" he said.

Tim said, "Well, was Wolf at school?"

"I didn't see him," said John.

"Yeah," Dean said. "I highly doubt it."

He pulled the car back into the road. "Okay then," he said, "we'll go by his place." He eyed Dean and Tim in the rearview mirror. "I still need your money," he said.

Light-hearted grumbling came from the backseat as a shower of two fives and a ten landed in his lap.

"Thanks," he said. "I get tired of buying for ya'll."

"I get so tired of buying for ya'll, blah blah blah..." came the playful, jeering voice of Tim.

"Aye, fuck you buddy!" Patrick said, doing his best Canadian *South Park* character voice.

Dean was quiet. He was thinking about the upcoming trip. He was thinking about the Goatman. He still hadn't had a chance to tell the guys what he had read the night before.

They pulled into the Fox Chase subdivision, found Wolf's house and pulled into his driveway.

Patrick gathered the money and added his own and John's, totaling forty dollars. "You guys are coming with me, you know," he said.

Uproar filled the car.

"Come on, man," Dean shouted. "We don't know him like that!" Tim and John nodded in agreement.

His fingers twisted and gripped on the steering wheel. He turned in his seat to face everyone. "I don't give a shit about that! I'm tired of dealing with him on my own. He already offered us the deal, he's not going to back out when you guys walk in. You guys always want to enjoy, but you never want to go any further."

John said "Well, we do throw in money, you know."

"You're coming," Patrick said as he got out of the seat and shut the door. The rest of them got out of the car slowly.

They shuffled sluggishly towards the doorway, knowing the rest of their day would be confusing, and most likely, terrifying.

He raised his hand to press the doorbell when they heard a sound.

Pssst.

Looking above them, they saw where the sound had come from. Wolf was standing in an open window. He began to lower a metal ladder out of the window onto the ground between John and Tim.

Wolf was wearing a Slipknot shirt and big pants with chains hanging from them. All black. His hair was in dreads.

The ladder clanged on the concrete driveway, and Dean mumbled something about how there was no way.

"Quit being a bitch," Patrick muttered.

Wolf said, "You guys have the forty dollars, right?"

"Yeah, we got the money, but why are we climbing into your house like firemen rescuing old ladies?" Tim said.

"Bro," Wolf said. "D'ya want the shit or not?"

They wanted the shit.

One by one, they climbed the ladder until they were all inside the room. Wolf's bedroom was a room above the garage of his mom's house. He pointed to his door. "I had a lock put on the door," he said. "To keep my bitch of a mom out." He pointed to a cordless phone in the corner. "And that right there is my personal phone line. Had it installed so I could handle business in private. Turns out my mom's boyfriend works for the cable company, so— free shit."

Patrick had been in here many times, but the other three boys looked around the room in amazement. The ceiling was slanted on two sides, running up to the roof. Along the walls were dozens of posters showcasing metal bands and obscure movies. Wolf had a large flat-screen television and a huge collection of games and movies. In the corner of the room stood a bookshelf with little metal tins on the shelves and incense burning in a glass holder. There were wall-mounted speakers in all four corners of the room, and Rob Zombie was blasting over the speakers, yelling about digging through the ditches and burning through the witches.

"This is awesome," said John.

"Yeah," agreed Tim and Dean in unison.

It was pretty cool, thought Patrick. *If not a little bit lame. I mean who still listened to Disturbed?*

He turned away and rolled his eyes. He thought that they wouldn't think it was so cool in a few minutes.

Wolf began pulling bean-bag chairs out from the closet and placing them around the room.

He picked the bag closest to him and plopped down hard in the most anticipatory fashion. It was a gesture that said let's just get this over with.

Wolf looked at Patrick, then turned to stare at the other three. Dean looked at Wolf in wide-eyed confusion.

"Don't you know you're being rude, man?" Wolf asked Dean.

"I'm sorry?"

"Don't be sorry, just sit down. Shit, you treat all your hosts with such disrespect?"

Sitting, Tim said, "I think you've got us wrong man, we, Wolf, it's just that we didn't know. We're sitting. Right, guys?"

Dean and John looked sheepish as they sat down in their chairs.

"Pat," Wolf said. "I'm assuming your friends are more of the meet the guy in the bathroom at school and toss the bud and the money under the stalls type. But as you know, I always let everyone test my product. I think of it as a courtesy. I mean, where else can you test something out for free before you buy it?"

Patrick thought, *car dealerships, gym member-ships, oh I could go on.* He kept these thoughts to himself, though.

"We appreciate this," said Tim.

"Yeah, man," John said. "Thank you."

Wolf walked over to the bookshelf and opened one of the metal tins. He pulled out a fist-sized chunk of fuzzy green marijuana. "Now, as Patrick will tell you, I'm very generous with my bud. I don't fuck with those little glass pipes or coke cans or none of that hobo shit. I make blunts, and I make 'em loud. So, sit the fuck down, and get ready."

Tim looked around just to be sure he wasn't crazy, and they were all indeed already sitting the fuck down except for Wolf.

"Will we be here a long time?" Dean said. "I've got supper at five."

Patrick shot Dean a look.

Wolf finished rolling the hefty blunt and began running his tongue up and down the sides of the paper, his tongue ring bobbed up and down. John saw this and thought he was going to puke.

Wolf stuck the blunt in his mouth and lit the end of it with a match from the shelf. The tip lit up a bright orange as he inhaled. He sucked in deeply, and after a few seconds, he blew the smoke out of his mouth, filling the room. The smell of it was terrible and amazing at the same time.

Finally, Wolf walked over to Patrick and handed him the blunt. He took it, said thank you, and began to inhale. Turning to Dean, Wolf said, "Don't worry about supper, man."

Dean, unsure of what to say, just nodded and said "Okay."

Patrick began coughing violently and passed the blunt to Tim, who was sitting on his left. Then Tim passed it to Dean, and Dean passed it to John.

After everyone had taken their turn with the blunt and the resulting coughing fit, Wolf went to the stereo and began playing some spacey instrumental music.

Patrick was floating already. He looked to his left and saw Tim slowly bobbing his head from side to side, his eyes glazed.

"Good shit, huh?" Wolf asked.

The four of them mumbled in agreement, and Wolf began to laugh hysterically. "You guys can't even fucking think!"

Wolf pulled up his own chair and sat down and began to explain the intricacies of unlocking the full potential of your mind.

Here we go, thought Patrick. *Always some stupid bullshit.*

Dean sunk down in his chair and stared at the ceiling. A poster for Slipknot's album, IOWA was on the slanted ceiling opposite him. The poster prominently displayed a sinister looking black goat.

Wolf saw Dean staring up at the poster. "You like that album?" he asked.

"What?" Dean's voice seemed to come from someone else.

"Do you like that album? You a Slipknot fan?" Every word seemed to reverberate around the room.

"Oh," Dean said. "No, not particularly. I guess I just wondered what the deal was with the goat."

Wolf lit another blunt and inhaled. "Well," he said, "the goat is supposed to symbolize the face of the Devil. Some call him Baphomet." He said all of this so matter-of-factly that it was obvious he felt proud of his knowledge.

Dean relaxed in his chair and closed his eyes, trying his hardest not to think of the Goatman.

CHAPTER SEVEN

After his bags were packed, Patrick was asked by his mother to go over his story once more. He told her that he and the other boys were going on a church trip to Tennessee. There was a church trip, but the boys wouldn't be attending. After their parents had forked over the money for the trip, each of them were supposed to take it—along with the permission form—to the church on a Wednesday night meet. Instead, the boys had gone to Wal-Mart and purchased camping gear and snacks. The only problem with their plan was in the assumption that none of their parents would talk to the Youth Minister at the church, Garrett Jones. It was a risk they took, understanding the consequences, but the boys felt certain it wouldn't be a problem. None of their parents could stand 'Brother Garrett,' as they found him pretentious and judgmental.

Patrick stood in the kitchen and talked excitedly to his mom about how they were going to be going into the slums and ministering to unfortunate children. When his mother's face showed a look of suspicion, he toned down the excitement a bit and instead shifted the conversation into a different direction, recalling all the pretty girls they had seen last year, and how Brother Garrett let them stay up as late as they wanted. This seemed to satisfy her.

Dean and Tim had both been dropped off at his house that Saturday morning around eight o'clock. The plan was to get to the campground around lunchtime and have plenty of daylight to set up their tents and get wood for a fire. Their parents, however, only knew the bus to

Tennessee was leaving at ten o'clock and, for whatever reason, the boys wanted to arrive together.

Kids were weird.

When Gary Hall walked outside to get the paper, the three boys were busy trying to shove all their bags into the tiny trunk of Patrick's Tempo. Amused, he stood for a moment watching them, and then he took a sip of his coffee, set it down, and walked over to the three of them.

"Wow," he said. "Did you guys all bring your dancin' shoes or what?"

Patrick's face reddened. It was way too much stuff for a church trip.

"They're having a talent show," Dean spoke up. "And so, I told the guys they should bring some stuff, I don't know, just for fun. You know, like guitars and stuff. Sorry Mr. Hall, I guess we should have thought it through a little more." He smiled.

Gary didn't know what to say. How do you tell teenage kids not to participate in church events?

"Oh, come on Dean, I'm only kidding," Gary said. "You guys take as much stuff as you need. But, you may want to take the Suburban, Patrick. I can drive your car a couple days."

"Really, dad? You don't have to—"

"Take it. Like I said, there's no law saying I can't drive my old Tempo around, is there?"

Patrick was flustered. If he took the Suburban, his dad could more easily find out where they really went. What if the campground is muddy and the Suburban gets too dirty? What if they took it to a car wash before returning it and it comes back too clean? What if his dad checks the mileage? It was too late for all that now.

"Thanks, Dad!" was all he said.

"Where the hell is John?" Patrick said a few minutes after his father had gone back inside and they had moved their bags to the Suburban.

"Don't look at us," Tim said. "That's your boy."

Dean laughed.

"What does that mean?"

"I'm just saying, if someone is going to know where he's gonna be, it's you. Can you argue with that?"

He thought about it. "No, I guess not," he said with a laugh.

"Has anyone called him?" said Tim.

"Yeah, three times," he said. "Okay," he continued, "we need to go get him, I guess." We're supposed to be at the church soon, and my mom is looking at us through the blin—don't fucking look!"

Dean and Tim had both turned to look.

"Jesus," Patrick said. "Let's go get him."

Tim called shotgun and climbed in the front seat of the Suburban. Dean climbed in the back. Patrick went inside to tell his mother that John needed them to come get him. After a minute, he returned to find the back of the Suburban had been left open. Grumbling, he shut it and climbed in the driver's seat.

<hr />

The night before he was supposed to leave for Coheelee Creek with his friends, John had been lying in bed thinking. Not of the upcoming trip, but of how badly he wanted to expose Ronnie as the snake he truly was. It made John sick to watch his poor mother get treated that way. He felt sure that if she knew about Ronnie stealing so much money from him, she would break it off for good. They could get assistance if it came to that, but by God, she deserved better.

The next morning, as he was getting ready for the trip, John could hear his mother and Ronnie arguing loudly in the living room. He zipped up his pack, grabbed his Atlanta Falcons hat, and walked down the hall and stood just outside the door to the living room.

"How could you be so stupid?" Ronnie said.

John's fists clenched.

"I'm sorry," his mother said. "It must have been the antibiotics."

"I swear to God, woman, you fucked up big this time," Ronnie said, and from behind cover, John watched him raise his hand against her.

"Don't fucking think about it!" John screamed, coming from behind the wall, his fists still clenched.

"John," his mother said with a shaky voice. "Don't talk to your—don't talk to Ronnie like that!"

"My what? My father?" He pointed at Ronnie. "This rat mother fucker is not my father."

Ronnie backed away from her and lunged across the room towards John.

"Ronnie!" John's mother screamed.

Ronnie crossed the living room in two large strides and pinned John against the wall with one hand, lifting John three inches off the ground and tearing a hole in his Fight Club t-shirt. John looked over his shoulder at his mother's desperate, yet sadly apathetic, facial expression.

Before giving Ronnie a second to speak, threaten him in some way, John brought his knee up into Ronnie's balls so hard that he could feel them move through his pants. Screaming, Ronnie dropped John, and John picked up his bag and ran out the front door.

———⊙———

Patrick had only just turned the Suburban onto John's street when he saw him. John was walking with a large backpack on his back and another bag in his hand. He looked upset. Patrick pulled up next to him and tapped the horn. Startled, John didn't recognize the vehicle at first, but once he realized who it was, he quickly climbed in the back seat and tossed his bags into the back.

"Thanks," John said.

"What happened, man?" he asked. "We've been waiting on—" and then he put the pieces together. Ronnie. Something had happened with Ronnie. "Never mind that, you ready for this trip?"

"Hell yeah. I'm ready to get away from here. Maybe forever."

Dean smiled at John. "I feel you on that one."

Patrick put the Suburban on the highway headed toward Georgia, and the trip was under way.

CHAPTER EIGHT

Those boys were on their way to the greatest horror Early County has ever seen. I've since been asked if I believe in fate. Was that the only explanation for how things could have turned out the way they did? All I can say about that with any real certainty is that those boys must have done some terrible things in a previous life, if, of course, you follow that line of thinking. Me, I reckon it falls on Early County and the state of Georgia somewhat, being so ignorant to it. The newspapers said that it had been right in front of our eyes. How could we have missed it? To be honest, I've thought about that every day for the past twelve years. I've thought about what I'll say if'n when I go on this talk show. But I do know this: those woods are evil. Be it the cause or the product, I don't know. But there's forces out there that I can't explain. And of course, that goddamned Goatman.

Once the boys had made it safely out of the city limits without being spotted by anyone they knew, Patrick pulled the Suburban into a gas station to top off the tank.

Opening his door, Tim said, "I just find it so hard to believe that we have to sneak around like this just to go camping. I mean, I know we're gonna get blazed out there, but our parents don't have to know all the details."

"I know," Patrick said, picking up the handle on the gas pump and putting it into the tank. "But like I've said, my mom would never let me go if she knew where we were going."

"Mine either," John said.

"But why?" asked Tim. "What's the big deal?"

Patrick shrugged. "Afraid it's not safe I guess. Plus, there are rumors that sexual predators go out there a lot."

"You're saying that wrong," John said. "The rumors are that gay men go out there to screw. Like at the Westgate trail."

"Whatever."

Dean stood off to the side, arms folded. In truth, he was actually kind of scared after reading what he had about the covered bridge and the Goatman. He opened his mouth to speak, to tell the rest of them what he knew but, ultimately, he changed his mind, deciding that it wasn't the time for that.

The gas pump clicked off and Patrick went inside to pay with John trailing him. Dean and Tim looked at each other.

"Wonder if they're gonna screw," Tim said.

"You're sick," Dean said, laughing.

The Suburban headed east on Highway 52, and the tunes were blasting. Patrick had plugged his iPod into the sound system and the current song was *Freak on a Leash* by Korn. The boys sang karaoke to the song shamelessly.

In a pause between songs, John thought he heard a thump come from behind his seat. He looked at Dean, and said "Did you hear that?"

"Hear what?"

"I don't know, a thump." John turned around, but he couldn't see anything besides all their bags, which were stacked so high that it was impossible to see out of the back window. Glancing over their bags, John did see something that caught his eye. A book that he had loaned

Patrick months ago was shoved into the side pocket of Patrick's bag—*Lullaby* by Chuck Palahniuk.

"Hey Pat," John said. "Did you ever finish *Lullaby*?"

Patrick turned around slightly to see what John was talking about. "Oh yeah, man, I brought it to give it back to you. Sorry it took so long, I'm terrible at remembering shit."

"What did you think?" Dean asked.

"It wasn't *Fight Club*, that's for sure. But it was still really interesting." Patrick said. "Like, it started out strong, but the finish was kinda dumb."

"I guess I get what you're saying," John said. "I should have brought you *Survivor*. That one is awesome."

"Yes!" Said Tim. "I love that one."

Dean said, "Can I see that book?"

"Sure," John said, reaching into the pocket of the bag and handing him the book.

"Thanks," he said. He opened the book and began reading.

After some time—and a large sum of heartily sung karaoke songs—the boys reached the Chattahoochee river.

"This is it," Patrick said. "Once we cross this bridge, we're in Georgia."

Tim started singing "Way down yonder on the Chattahoochee... something, something... hairy coochie!" He laughed as if it were the funniest thing anyone had ever said.

Dean found a slip of paper on the seat next to him and shoved it into his book. "Do we need to get anything from a store?" he asked. "Cause I don't want to have to leave once we get there."

Patrick stared forward in concentration. "Yeah," he said. "But I think we may have passed them all."

"No," John said. "There's a little gas station right where we turn on the left. I mean it's a real Texas Chainsaw Massacre type of place, but you can buy shit there."

The bridge was long, and the water was blinding, shining reflective rays off the sun. Patrick thought the water looked amazing. He wondered if the water at Coheelee Creek would look that good.

Shortly after having crossed the bridge, he saw the road the gas station was on and pulled the Suburban into a parking spot. "This is it," he said. "Last chance to buy whatever you want."

They all piled out of the vehicle and gazed at the building. It was a very old place; the wood paneling was mostly rotted and peeling back. The windows had bars across them, and out by the road, there was a single gas pump.

He led the way inside, and the other three followed him. Immediately upon entering the building, the smell of cigar smoke knocked them back like a wave.

The man behind the counter looked up from his paper at the crowd of teenagers. "Whatcha need?"

"Oh, hey," John spoke up. "We're just getting some food, thank you." He sounded nervous.

"Need any milk?" The sweaty man in the stained wife-beater asked.

"Milk?" John said.

"You fuckin' deaf?"

"No sir," Patrick said. "I don't think we need any milk." Dean and Tim exchanged glances that said let's hurry and get out of here.

The group hastily found what they wanted: energy drinks, candy, and other small things they hadn't thought to pack (or rather, didn't have a chance to) and approached the counter.

"Sure you don't want no milk? That's what most people come in here want. We got the best milk you'll ever drink. Has healing powers, so they say." He pointed to a small cooler next to the counter stocked with mason jars filled with milk.

"I'm pretty sure," he said, glancing at the jars filled with the white liquid. It didn't look like regular cow's milk to him. Maybe goat milk? He decided he didn't want to know.

"Thas' ok," the man said. "Where you boys headed?"

"Camping," Dean said abruptly. The man looked taken aback.

"Goin' t'see the ole covered bridge, are we? Maybe try to find that crazy old Goatman?" He laughed a strange smoker's ramble and began coughing harshly, spit flying everywhere.

Patrick was growing impatient. "How much do I owe you?"

The man looked at all the items in one sweeping glance. "Eighteen bucks'll do," he said, stifling more coughs.

Patrick dropped two tens down on the counter and turned for the door. He wasn't worried about his change. He just wanted to get the fuck out of there.

Once they were all outside, he asked, "What the hell is the goat man?"

"I'll tell you later," Dean said.

Using the wireless key fob to unlock the doors, the group were in the process of getting into the Suburban when they heard a noise. A large semi-truck was careening down the road and had locked up the brakes. The trailer attached to the cab was swaying from left to right in quick violent jerking motions.

"Holy shit!" Tim yelled. "It's gonna tip over!"

Dean turned and looked across the street. He had seen movement in the trees.

"Run!" Patrick screamed as the trailer flipped on its side and began scraping the asphalt and gravel, sliding towards the gas station. The four boys scrambled as far away as they could and watched in horror as the trailer took out the single gas pump. Liquid spewed out in all directions, but there was no fire, no explosion. The pump significantly slowed the trailer, and it stopped to a dead halt three feet from the back of Gary Hall's prized Suburban.

Several seconds passed before anyone said anything. Finally, in a panicked voice, Patrick said, "We have to leave... now."

"Leave?" John said. "We can't leave! We have to see if the driver is okay. We have to know what happened. We have to—"

"The cops will be here any minute!"

"Exactly! They'll want to talk to witnesses."

"Right, John. They'll want to talk to us. To bring a camera crew and interview us, so they can put it on the fucking six o'clock news, so fucking Ronnie can watch it with his dinner and come out here and kill you. Or worse, send you to that boot camp he's always talking about."

Behind him, Dean and Tim exchanged glances. John stood still with his fists clenched, fighting back tears. He knew Patrick was right, but it didn't make what he'd said hurt any less. Patrick's face had an expression that said I'm sorry, but you know it's true.

"Yeah," John said. "Okay, let's go."

CHAPTER NINE

Sheriff Paul Stanton sat on the john reading the classified ads. *Someone's trash is someone else's future trash*, he thought. There were advertisements for old cars, piano lessons, and of course, free kittens. But there was something else too.

Something odd.

'Have you seen the Goatman?' read the title of an advertisement spot, followed by:

'Don't look into his eyes.'

And that was all. "Who pays for this shit?" Stanton said aloud to the empty room as he set down the paper and reached for the toilet paper. Just as he was standing to pull his pants up, there was a knock on the door.

"The hell is it?"

"Sir, there's a problem."

"I'm shittin', Benny. For Christ's sake!"

He could hear the deputy sigh from the other side of the door.

"Sir, I'm sorry, but an eighteen-wheeler went and smashed into Floyd's Market."

He opened the bathroom door. "Is anyone hurt?"

"We don't know for sure. Floyd said there was some kids who'd come in his store and was leavin' when it happened. Says the trailer damn near turned 'em into hot cakes."

"But they're okay?" he asked as he strode across the room to grab his hat and keys.

"That's what I'm saying, sir. They've left. He said they was some shady boys, acting funny the whole time they was in his store. And he says they just left after the crash, like they was running from the Devil, he says."

He picked up his insulated mug of coffee and took a sip, noting that it was strange to hold something metal in his left hand without it clacking against his ring. Thank Susan for that. Susan and her goddamn drinking problem. Susan and her credit card maxing. Susan and her fucking other men.

"Sir?" Benny said.

He blinked. "Yeah. Yeah. Let's go. We can take my car."

———◦———

Paul pulled his cruiser into the far side of the parking lot, and they got out and surveyed the scene.

"These good-for-nothin' reporters!" Benny snarled. "How do they beat us to everything?"

He thought, *I'm shittin', Benny*, but instead he said, "I have no idea. Honestly it makes me wonder sometimes whether they are the ones causing the problems."

Just then the owner of the gas station, Floyd, walked around the corner of the building, waving his hands in the air. "Over here!" he called. "I'm the owner! Over here!"

"Damnit Floyd, we know who you are," he called. "There ain't but two gas stations in this town, and you got one of 'em here."

Benny tried to put on his best Serious Deputy stare but found it hard to keep a straight face after Stanton's outburst. The sheriff wasn't a man of many words. In fact, in the years he had worked under him, he had come to find that he seemed to (subconsciously or otherwise) pick and choose carefully the words he would say, as if he had a daily limit he was afraid of approaching. There it would be, six o'clock at night, the phone rings, and he couldn't say anything because, damnit, he just talked too much at work and crossed a threshold. In most cases, a mere grunt might replace a word as simple and non-taxing as yes. It just seemed that Stanton had just used up his daily quota. It was no secret that Paul didn't care much for Floyd or his, in Stanton's words, hick-ass market. They'd had their run-ins.

"Well, are ya gonna just yell at me, or are ya gonna do somethin', Sheriff?"

Benny interrupted, "Floyd, is the driver okay? What exactly happened?"

"Yeah," Floyd said, swatting at a fly. "Driver seemed okay. He went unconscious just before they took him off, but before he passed out, he kept screaming something over and over."

"What's that?"

Floyd stuck his thumbs under his denim overalls straps and turned his head and spat.

"Goat man."

Nobody said anything for a long time. Finally, he said, "Tell me about these kids, Floyd."

<hr>

After leaving the gas station, the ride to the campground was less than ten minutes. Patrick had sped away from the Floyd's Market rather quickly, hoping to miss any emergency vehicles or news crews.

"This is so fucked up!" Tim shouted. "We should be back there checking on that driver. We just fled the scene of an accident. That's against the law, isn't it?"

"No," Patrick said. "We didn't break any laws. It wasn't like a hit and run. That's what you're thinking of. We just happened to see a truck tip over; we didn't cause it."

In the back seat, Dean had his face in John's copy of *Lullaby* by Chuck Palahniuk. He had felt nervous ever since Floyd's mention of the Goatman, and he found that reading calmed him, so he read.

Patrick continued, "You guys do realize that the guy who ran that store has a phone, right? He probably called 9-1-1 before we even left the lot."

"Yeah, I know," Tim said. "Still don't make it right." And he was done discussing the matter.

"Turn left here," John said.

He turned the vehicle onto a dusty dirt road.

"Just about a mile down here is the turn."

"Finally," Tim said. "First order of business, I'm getting baked. I've never been this nervous in my life."

Patrick said, "Nobody's getting baked until we have all of our stuff set up. Also, we need to gather wood."

"I can walk and chew gum at the same time," Tim sneered.

"Turn here," John said, as they approached the sign which read: *Coheelee Creek Covered Bridge*. A smaller sign below this one read: *Campers, Please Be Courteous*.

Patrick parked the Suburban in front of the wooden fencing near the campgrounds. They all got out, stretched their legs and admired the scenery. Down the sloping hill sat the campground among few trees and behind that ran the creek. The water in the creek was clear and sparkling in the treacherous Georgia heat. To the right, the creek ran down into a series of small rivers, a few waterfalls, and a larger river. To the left was the famous covered bridge.

They began unpacking the Suburban and taking their things down the hill to the camping area. Dean was reaching in the back of the vehicle to grab the tent when he saw their bags shuffling around on their own. Jumping back, he called for Patrick, who was standing in front of the car with his hands on his hips, proud to finally be free, if only for a weekend.

"What is it?" he asked.

Dean backed away and pointed to the rear of the vehicle. Patrick came around to look while Tim and John dropped what they were carrying to come and see what was wrong.

He leaned into the back of the Suburban apprehensively, like a dog meeting a stranger. The tent shifted and fell, and a hand emerged from beneath. The four of them jumped back, cursing.

"Don't hurt me," said a small voice, and Patrick, in complete shock and disbelief, knew immediately who it was.

Sam.

CHAPTER TEN

S mall, fetal, and sad looking, Sam lay in the back of the Suburban among the bags and boxes.

"What are you doing?" Patrick roared. "Oh my God, Sam—Mom and Dad are going to kill me!"

The other three boys stood frowning but said nothing.

Sam pulled his way out from below the bags and brushed himself off. He stood looking at the four of them, tears welling in his eyes. "I'm sorry," he said. "But you don't have to worry about Mom and Dad. I told them I was going with you, to that church thing. I told her you invited me, and she was so excited... I asked her not to mention it because it would embarrass you." Sam's gaze met his brother's, and they both looked down, blushing.

"Sam, I—"

"I should have just asked you if I could come. I was just afraid that you'd say no. But you know I'm cool. You know that whatever you guys came to do, I'm cool with it. But Patrick... I need this."

Patrick thought back on the year his little brother had just endured. He had been molested by some of his peers, ridiculed, tripped, called a homo on a daily basis, shoved into lockers, and had been the recipient of more than one old-fashioned ass-whooping. Not to mention all the doctors he'd had to see over the foot-dragging phase.

He really does need this, he thought.

"You stay right here," Patrick said, pointing to Sam. He motioned for the other three to follow him, and he walked a good distance away from the Suburban.

They all gathered in a small circle, except for Sam, who was still standing by the car. "Look," he said to them. "I know this sucks, and it's lame, and I'm sorry. But we should really just give him a chance. You guys know what he's been through, I think we should let him have this."

None of them spoke. Tim began nodding slowly, and John and Dean followed.

"It's okay with me," said John. "I mean, we don't have much of a choice now, but still, Sam is cool. Let's just start getting our shit set up before it's dark."

And so, they did. Collectively, they dragged the cooler full of drinks down by their chosen campsite area (a recently used and enjoyed patch near the creek with a small campfire still set up). Tim and Dean worked together to gather wood from the nearby woods while the others worked on the tent.

"So much of this whole ordeal is extremely dependent on the small chance that we won't overlook some major flaw," said John. "I mean if we do so much as put the tent back in the box wrong—"

"It's done," Patrick said. "Quit worrying about it. Even if we do get in trouble, so what? We've been wanting to do this for so long, let's enjoy it while we're here, or let's go home and tell our parents God cancelled our field trip."

◦

They started a fire just before it began to get dark. There were only four chairs, so Sam was left to sit on a large rock that Patrick had found for him. Forming a semi-circle around the fire, they sat with Sam on the end next to Patrick. He thought about offering Sam his chair, because he felt that it was the right thing to do, but ultimately, he brushed away the idea, reminding himself that no one had forced Sam to come along like a prisoner trying to escape on the produce truck.

Dean was slow to come to the fire, sitting in the tent with a flashlight and his book.

"What are you doing, man?" Tim called in the direction of the tent.

Dean clicked off the flashlight and crawled out of the opening to the tent looking perplexed, like something was on his mind. "I've just read the craziest thing in that Palahniuk book. You know the hippie guy? When he says the part about the bait cow?"

"Oh yeah," said Patrick. "Shit is screwed up." He noticed Sam glance up at the word shit, but the younger boy quickly turned away and tried his best to appear totally cool with it.

"What are you guys talking about?" John said. "I don't remember any cow."

Dean said, "The guy is explaining the cattle industry. He says there's a cow who's trained to lead the other cattle into the slaughter room." Dean swallowed. "It's like she's saying 'follow me this way, it's okay.' But it's not okay. They get slaughtered. And in the end, the bait cow gets slaughtered, too."

"Do you think that's true?" Sam said in his small voice.

"I'm sure it could be," replied Patrick. "But it is kind of hard to believe that a cow could be trained to do that. Who would want to do that? To lead others to their death on a regular basis?"

Tim stood up. "It's too early for all this crazy shit-talking, man. Where's the weed?"

Patrick and Sam exchanged glances. Sam zipped the imaginary zipper built into his lips. "I swear," he said.

He reached reluctantly into his bag and pulled out the sack of weed they had bought from Wolf. Tim finished the Coke he was drinking and crushed the can carefully, making a small valley in the aluminum. Then he reached down and pulled a safety pin out of the tongue of his shoe and used it to poke a dozen or so holes in the aluminum valley. "Load it up, Pat," he said.

And while the five of them sat around the fire, something sat in the woods and watched them.

Sam declined his brother's offer to puff from the can when it came to be his turn. Sam's curiosity was strong, but he saw something in his brother's eyes when he offered him the can which said, *I'm only offering to appear nice.* He caught his brother's's drift. He was lucky enough to have come with them; he would do well not to overstep his boundaries.

After the four older boys were good and high, they set out to make some dinner.

"You know what I could go for?" Tim said while he and John set up a small spread of snack food on a nearby rock. "An ice-cold beer," he said, after no one asked him.

"Oh bullshit," Dean said. "Beer tastes like hot garbage, and you know it. That's what you told me. You said beer wouldn't taste any worse if it was funneled from a homeless man's asshole." There was laughter from the others at that.

Tim blushed. "Well, I think I might could change my mind. You don't know. Besides, it's not about the taste. I wanna get drunk."

"Getting drunk is lame," Dean said. "Terrible for your health and just genuinely dangerous. Weed is way safer," Dean said.

"I know," Tim said. "I just want to see what the fuss is all about."

After eating, they discussed what they wanted to do the next day. The morning would be for gathering firewood, the afternoon for swimming and exploring.

"Aren't you guys just a little bit scared being out here at night?" John said. "I mean, I know we came knowing what they say about this place, but I just feel creeped out. Just me?"

"No," Dean said. "It's not just you." And he decided to finally tell them what he had read on the internet about the Goatman.

He talked for ten minutes straight while the other four (Sam especially) sat in silent, apprehensive horror.

John leaned forward in his chair and said, "We have to find the noose."

"Right now?" Dean replied. "No way!"

"Yeah," Patrick said. "I'm absolutely not going out there in the dark."

"Pussies. All of you," said John.

None of them replied. The fire popped.

He continued. "Well, we at least have to go to the bridge. It's just up the hill, I can see it from here."

"But what about the Goatman?" Sam said.

Patrick laughed nervously. "It's a load of crap," he said. "There is no such thing."

Sam wasn't convinced, but he nodded anyway.

They all found their flashlights and reluctantly followed John up the hill toward the bridge.

Tim struggled up the hill complaining that his leg had fallen asleep. "What are you gonna tell us next, Dean?" He said. "That the Goatman is also part spider, and he's got all his fucking spider-goat-man babies in a web in the corner of the bridge?"

"The hanging didn't even happen on the bridge," Dean said. "It's just an old historic landmark. There's only so many of these things in the world or something."

A tree cracked in the woods, and the sound echoed all along the creek bed, causing them all to jump. Looming just yards away from them was the bridge. The size of it. The old thing creaked in the wind. They approached it, shining their flashlights.

"What is the point of coming up here?" Patrick asked.

"You scared?" said John.

"No, I just don't know why we can't come back in the morning."

A small voice came from inside the covered bridge. It seemed to utter a one syllable word: *hey*.

Sam screamed and started running down the hill toward the campfire. Patrick watched him go and then turned and ran toward the bridge with his flashlight out before him, bouncing light around like a flaccid penis pissing all over a toilet seat. John and Tim followed him, but Dean froze in place, his shoes seemingly stuck to the ground by some unimaginable force. His face scrunched into a grimace.

"Hello?" Patrick called.

A skittering noise like long nails on wood came from across the void. He shined his flashlight slowly from one dark corner to the next. Something moved overhead. Behind him stood John and Tim, both of whom had seemed to forget their flashlights entirely. Several yards behind them stood Dean, petrified.

"Who the fuck is out here with us?" John hissed. "A kid. I heard a kid. I know it."

"I don't even know if that's what I heard," said Tim. "Sounded more to me like some kind of animal. Like, maybe, do you think it was some kind of animal?"

"Like a goat?" Patrick said as he flashed the light around the darkness. "Please don't tell me you mean that."

Tim shuddered. "Actually, yeah."

⎯⎯⎯◦⎯⎯⎯

If interviewed just then, Sam would have had no problem telling anyone that he had fucked up royally by coming along on this trip. Panting when he reached the tent, he turned and looked over his shoulder to assure himself that no one bad was following him. No one at all, actually. Was it an over-reaction for him to bolt like he did? Were the other guys currently in trouble?

No, he could hear them talking. And shouting. The shouting is why they didn't see the figure like Sam did. The bridge is why they didn't see the hooded figure standing by the Suburban.

Sam screamed again.

CHAPTER ELEVEN

Stranger things had never happened to any of them in their lives, and no one slept very well that night. Not long after they returned to the campfire, they all piled into the tent and tried to get comfortable. Sam either had forgotten about the figure by the Suburban or had chosen to pretend he had. They were crammed into the tent, not having accounted for the fifth person in their original plans, and Dean, Tim, and John were annoyed even further by Sam's self-invitation. Patrick knew they were all upset and he felt that he should be, too, but he just couldn't bring himself to be angry over what his brother had done.

Dean was crammed into the corner of the tent, thankful that he wasn't in Tim's position, in the middle, crammed between two guys. The inside of the tent created its own kind of sick atmosphere, complete with the strong odor of sweaty socks.

"Well, this has been a shit trip," Dean said.

"What the hell was that back there?" asked Tim.

"I don't want to know," Patrick said.

Sam thought to himself and spoke up, "There's something I didn't say before, but I need to say it now because I don't think I can sleep unless someone makes me feel better about this."

Sam had everyone's attention. "When you guys were up at the bridge, I think I saw somebody standing by the car."

"Stop it," snapped his brother, trying not to sound shaken. "You're making it up for attention."

"I'm not! I swear. The person was all hunched over the car, and they were wearing a hood."

"Why didn't you say something before, then? Why wait until we're all crammed together in this hot ass tent?" Patrick struggled to get to the doorway.

"Don't go out there!" Sam yelped.

"Fuck that!" Tim said. "I'm not sitting in here waiting to get grabbed by some crazy bastard with a machete. I'm getting out of here."

At this point, the whole lot of them were stirring, putting on their shoes. Patrick exited the tent first. Sam was the last to exit.

John walked over to the fire and used a stick to poke some life back into it.

Dean produced some flashlights, and they started walking towards the Suburban.

"Wait," said John. "Shouldn't we leave a couple people here? You know, to make sure our stuff is okay?"

"Sure," Patrick said. "Does that mean you're volunteering?"

John's face tightened. "I don't care, sure."

"I'll stay here with you," Sam said, sitting on a rock with his back to the fire.

"Okay, we'll be right back," said Patrick as he and the others went to investigate.

———◦◦◦———

The Suburban wasn't far at all, but in the darkness at that very moment it seemed five miles away. Patrick thought that he should have listened to John when he said that they should bring a gun. Ronnie had a pistol that he probably wouldn't miss for a few days, but Patrick had told John no, simply because he thought a gun and marijuana didn't sound like the best idea. Right then, he'd take a redneck's entire arsenal with a smile on his face.

They reached the wooden fence in front of the grass parking lot and worked their legs over it. The Suburban seemed okay. The tires were okay, and it was still locked.

"I don't see anything," said Patrick. "Let's go back."

"Wait," Dean said as he pointed.

"Oh my God."

Patrick. Dean, and Tim stared at the back of the Suburban for a long time, none of them able to move. On the back of the otherwise spotless vehicle there were dozens of wet, muddy handprints.

CHAPTER TWELVE

Midnight. The fire burned high. Five nervous kids sat huddled by the flames. The three who had ventured to the vehicle had returned, looking a bit like their eyes could fall out of their sockets.

"What?!" John had demanded. "What is it? What happened? Tell me!"

"Someone is out here," Patrick said.

John blinked. Sam went inside the tent in such a quick manner, you would have thought there was a toilet in there.

"Or at least there *was* someone out here," said Dean.

"What's the difference?" Tim said. "We need to fucking get the hell out of here."

Patrick stepped up on one of the rocks, and all the attention shifted to him. He looked as if he were holding the conch in Golding's *Lord of the Flies*.

"Alright, here's the deal," he said. "Yes, what happened is weird. But it's most likely just some retarded local kids fucking with us. There was the noise at the bridge, and then the car. It's the type of shit we would do if we lived out here, and you know it. People from out of state come out here after hearing rumors online about the area being haunted, and the pranksters make it a reality. Hell, the only reality that really exists is probably the one they've made. And then, of course, you have the alternative to staying, going home and telling our parents why we're back early."

"I'm beyond that, dude," Dean said, his voice shaking. "I don't care anymore."

"What about John?" Patrick retorted. "Ronnie will run his face over with the fucking lawnmower!"

"Can we not talk about him right now?" John said, flustered.

Patrick crossed his arms. "At least, let's wait until morning. That's all I'm asking. It's late, we all know that. Most of us are pretty fucked up, and the only one who isn't can't even drive yet. This is a one-horse town, and you better believe he'll be sitting in the bushes on the highway waiting for some dumbass kids to bust. It's too risky."

No one had anything to say. An owl began hooting overhead. The fire had begun to burn down again; the coals whispered secrets to each other in flared excitement. Nature wasn't shy.

"I have an idea," Sam said from the entryway of the tent. "We could have a couple people stand guard for a couple hours and then rotate. Like they do in the movies. That will get us through until morning."

"And what happens when Jeepers Creepers runs out of the woods and starts calling us names?" Dean said. "We just have a wrestling match to the death by the creek?"

"I realize now that we should have brought a gun," admitted Patrick. "But we didn't. And it sucks. But I'm sure we will be fine. Now, I hate to ask this, but it has to be said. Who wants to volunteer to go first?"

"I think it should definitely be two people," said Tim.

"Yeah, In case one falls asleep."

"You know, I wasn't going to say this," Dean said. "But I think Sam should have to be on first watch."

Sam blushed. "I... I mean—"

"Why is that?" Patrick asked, his volume rising.

"You know why."

Patrick opened his mouth to say something but was interrupted.

"I was going to volunteer anyways," Sam said. "I don't know if I could sleep if I swallowed a whole bottle of sleeping pills."

"Okay," Dean said. "Good deal, then. Who else?"

"Maybe you should," said Patrick. "Give you a chance to apologize to Sam for being a dick."

Dean bowed his chest the slightest bit. John stepped between them, waving them off.

"Maybe you should stay out here so you can suck him off some more," Dean said. "So afraid to hurt his feelings, tell it like it is, Pat. Tell him how you're ashamed of him because he's a ball fondler. Tell him it was a shitty move forcing his way into our vacation."

Patrick looked from Dean—his supposed friend—to Sam—his little brother—and back to Dean and found himself speechless.

"Did you really say all of those things?" Sam demanded.

"No."

"Oh really?" Dean asked. "I seem to remember differently. I remember you coming to school after everyone found out what happened, embarrassed as hell. You said he was a fag, and that you didn't know how that happened in your family."

Before Patrick had a chance to say anything else, Tim intervened. "I'll sit on first watch with Sam," he said. "And honestly, I don't know what the hell is going on with you two, but it's shitty, and it needs to stop. Take your asses to sleep, and I'll wake you up in a couple hours."

Dean, Patrick, and Sam stood in a small circle, staring one another down for a few moments longer until eventually, Dean stormed into the tent, breaking the tension a bit.

Patrick said, "Sam, I'm sorry. I don't really feel that way. I've been very open with you about what I think."

Sam sat down in a chair close to the fire. He kicked some sticks into the coals and sighed. Without looking at his brother, he said, "I'll see you in a couple hours. Get some sleep."

———————◦◦———————

Tim and Sam sat outside the tent in awkward silence. Tim tried making small talk, but he didn't know that much about Sam except for the fact that he had been accused of being gay. How's that for casual conversation? They talked a little about the Goatman and the bridge, but when Tim noticed Sam getting noticeably bothered, he dropped the subject.

It wasn't long before Sam fell asleep in his chair, head cocked back, mouth open.

Oh wow, thanks, thought Tim. *I stand up for you, and you repay me by making me go this watch solo.*

What was worse, he had to piss. One thing about Sam falling asleep was that he wouldn't have to go far for privacy. He stood up slowly and walked over to the other side of the fire. He glanced around, as if someone might be out here who might see him, then he unzipped his pants and pulled out his penis. This is when most guys would just piss. But Tim wasn't like most guys. He did piss, that wasn't the problem. The problem was that he hadn't taken care of his "problem" in almost a whole day, which must have been some kind of record. Instead of putting himself back in his pants after he finished, he turned around and faced the fire, feeling the heat on his naked torso and groin. It drove him crazy. He wondered what Sam would think if he woke up and saw him standing there playing with himself, but then he thought that he'd probably like it, and he almost laughed out loud. Deep down, though, Tim had an animalistic urge, and he didn't give a fuck if anyone saw. In fact, a part of him wished they would.

He finished his business in a dizzying haste. The shame which usually followed this act came in waves, especially with Patrick's little brother just across the fire from him, but at least it was done.

He couldn't help but think of the time his mother had walked in on him; her reaction would never leave his mind. *You filthy little shit.*

Tim had the unshakable feeling of being watched. He glanced around, heart beating madly in his chest.

"Hello?" he called, feeling silly. There was no one out here but them, right?

He heard a small voice from just beyond the tree line. The voice said, "Hey."

CHAPTER THIRTEEN

Sam woke so suddenly and violently that he resembled a dying person who had been stabbed in the chest with a dose of adrenaline. He had been dreaming, or rather, having a nightmare. In it, he was wandering on a wooded path in search of something unknown, and he kept coming across bloody chunks of a human body. He followed the trail of gore for a long time, stumbling across a leg here, a nose there. All along the way was residue of a pinkish-white goo which looked like a giant snail's slime. Only instead of mucus, this trail appeared to consist of human (or some other animal) pieces ground into a paste.

Finally, he came to the end of the gory path, where his father was hunched over like Gollum from Tolkien's masterpiece. Gary Hall's eyes rolled absently in his skull, and he never appeared to actually look at Sam when he spoke.

"Well, would you just look at that," he said. "Look at it! Goddamnit, I didn't raise no faggot."

Sam tried to say something in protest to that remark, not realizing, of course, that he was in a dream. But he was unable to speak. He could only stand there and listen to his father belittle him.

"Look behind you."

Sam turned around and screamed in silent horror. The shock of it. His body was gone from the torso down, insides unraveling like a bloody kite string. Turning around, he faced his father. Gary had somehow immediately and silently closed the gap between them, until he was mere inches away from Sam's face. He could smell the stink of rot coming from all his orifices. His teeth were filed to jagged yellow points, and maggots writhed in his eye sockets.

"Do you see now what you are? You're just a diseased little cocksucker is all. I should have pulled out when I fucked your whore mother. But you know what? I couldn't stop myself. You understand, don't you?" And then Gary Hall opened his mouth and lunged towards him.

That was when Sam woke up.

———◦———

"You were supposed to wake us up after a couple hours," Patrick said. "The sun is already coming up. Have you been sleeping this whole time?"

"No. I don't know."

"Where is Tim?"

"I don't know."

His brother sighed. "Well what about the alarm? I thought he was setting an alarm on his phone?"

Before Sam could answer, John said, "I can't find my phone."

"Me neither," Dean said, rifling through his bag.

None of their phones could be found.

"We need to look for Tim," Patrick said. "He can't be far. Maybe he took our phones, you know, as a prank or something."

Each of them walked in a different direction from the campsite, shouting Tim's name over and over like rabid fans calling to their favorite actor walking by on the red carpet.

There was no answer.

Dean had begun to pace back and forth, mumbling to himself. "What the fuck is going on?" He said. "I can't see him taking our phones and hiding for a laugh."

"Why not?" asked Patrick.

"Because it's not funny."

They all agreed to sit down and eat some breakfast while they gathered their thoughts. Sam helped Patrick set out some snack foods from their bags, and each of them grabbed a bottle of water.

The food, for the most part, was picked at without much enthusiasm. The day was already shaping up to be very hot. The trees seemed to sweat in the southern heat. Patrick thought of what they had originally planned on doing today. Swimming in the not-so-secret whirlpools and jumping from the rope swing into the hundred-foot-drop below. That would have been cool and refreshing and fun.

Instead they would spend the day looking for their friend.

Their dumbass friend who was supposed to stay awake and on watch.

Dean stood up and tossed his food down. "I can't just keep sitting here," he said. "I know you guys think Tim is just messing with us, or maybe he just went off exploring or something, but I don't believe that, okay? This place is just... wrong. You all know it. We should have never come out here."

"I didn't see you arguing when we planned this trip," said Patrick, who also stood up.

"Don't start this shit again," John pleaded. "We'll go look for him right now."

Each of them threw their trash into the newly-lit fire and began to get their things together.

"I think we should leave someone here like last time," Sam said. "You know, with our stuff."

"Are you scared to go out there with us?" Patrick asked.

"No. I'm not scared. I'm just... I just have a bad feeling about leaving our stuff unwatched."

"It's daylight."

"Just let him stay if he wants to," Dean said. "It doesn't matter. He'll be fine."

————◦————

Patrick didn't feel right leaving Sam behind, but he did it anyway. He was so tired of trying to do what everyone wanted him to do, so tired of being the "leader." But it always happened this way, Patrick being in charge. It just came naturally. Only, sometimes, a leader needs a leader as well.

"He's always going on and on about the rope swing drop down at the river," Dean said. "We should check there first."

"This path here takes you right there," John said. "It Y's off to the right, and it's right down there."

As they walked, Dean couldn't stop thinking about the dreaded Goatman. It seemed like the very essence of the thing had crept into his soul. But why? He couldn't explain it, but ever since he had read what he found online, he hadn't had a moment awake—or asleep—where the legendary creature wasn't in his thoughts.

They made their way down the path until they came to the fork at the end.

"We go right here," John said.

They turned right, and Dean said, "I don't feel right about this place. I don't feel right about any of it. I think we should leave."

"I know how you feel," said Patrick. "But we have to find Tim. If this place is that bad, we can't just leave him out here."

"I know, but I don't think you understand. It's evil out here. If this place doesn't want us to find Tim, we won't."

"Bullshit," John said. "It's all bullshit. We'll find Tim, he's probably laughing at us right now. I wouldn't be surprised if he jumped out of the damn trees right now and mooned us."

They had reached the cliff with the rope swing. The rope swing was attached to a limb on an old oak tree that stood by the edge of the cliff. They walked over to the edge and looked down.

"Is this the part where Tim jumps out and says 'boo'?" Dean asked.

There was nothing at the bottom of the cliff besides the river which looked very deep. The drop looked to be at least three stories down.

"I've jumped it once," John said. "It's pretty insane. Your balls feel like they're being pulled off when you land though."

"That's great," Patrick said. "We need to head back, keep looking in some other direction."

They turned around and started to head back to camp. Then there was a noise.

"What is that?" Patrick shouted.

The Suburban was blasting down the path in a furious roar, the engine being pushed to its limit. Small trees were pummeled under the vehicle as it drifted lazily towards the group of them.

Patrick and John darted towards the woods on the left, and the Suburban continued on its path. Dean was standing directly in its way. Both Patrick and John were shouting for him to get the hell out of the way, and he finally did move, just in time, but not before he thought he had seen a figure in the driver's seat. The figure of a goat.

The entire driver's side of the Suburban scraped against the rope-swing-tree, and then it continued right off the cliff and landed in the river.

CHAPTER FOURTEEN

Of course, there hadn't been any goat behind the wheel of the Suburban. At least that's what Patrick and John told Dean. They told him that there must have been a huge stick slammed between the driver's seat and the gas pedal. They said how there was probably duct tape holding the steering wheel straight. But he wasn't convinced.

Patrick started shouting about how they had to make sure Sam was okay. He couldn't believe they had been dumb enough to leave him alone in the first place.

Running back up the trail towards the camp, they heard voices coming from the woods. Dean thought it was his imagination again, but he saw that the others had heard it, too.

"Tim!" John yelled. "Where are you? Is that you?"

Silence.

"Come on," Patrick shouted at them. "Back to camp!"

Patrick could feel his heart beating in his chest so hard that his shirt was pulsing outward with its rhythm. *I can't lose Sam out here*, he thought. *I might as well just follow the Suburban off that cliff head first.*

They reached the point where the trail opened back into the campgrounds and, panting, they searched for Sam and Tim.

"Sam!" Patrick shouted to no avail. He could see that the campgrounds were bare. There was no sign that anyone had been there at all, save for the smoldering fire and some small bits of trash strewn about.

He walked over to the stumps by the fire and sat down, putting his face in his hands.

"I knew we shouldn't have come out here," Dean said, shaking his head and looking off past the creek.

"What, because you had a fucking dream?" John said.

"Shut the fuck up," Patrick said, visibly shaken. "I have to think."

"I don't have to think," Dean said. "I know which way the road is."

Patrick stood up and walked over to Dean, getting close enough to kiss him. "You do what you need to do," he said. "But I'm not leaving here without my brother. And maybe you forgot, but your best friend is out here somewhere too. But like I said, do what you have to do."

"Pat," John said. "We could go get help."

"From who? The only person I've seen within miles of this place is that gas station owner and he looked like a fucking rapist. I'm not leaving until I find Sam."

"It's not your fault that he came along," Dean reminded him.

"I'm going to find him. You can come with me or you can leave, I don't care."

John and Dean exchanged glances and nobody spoke for a minute or so. Finally, Dean said, "Which way should we go?"

⸺⸺⸺◆⸺⸺⸺

The three boys searched the area around the campground thoroughly, but the only useful thing they found was a small cigarette lighter. Patrick put the lighter in his pocket, and the group headed back down the path towards the heart of the woods.

"What are we looking for?" said John.

"Anything," Patrick said. "Just anything, I don't know." He began to sob.

Dean said, "Hey man. I'm sorry, okay? It was a dick move to—"

"I don't care what you said or did!" Patrick shouted. "Aren't you guys scared? My brother and our friend are both missing, and someone pushed my dad's Suburban off a cliff! What the fuck?"

"I'm terrified," Dean said. "That's why I tried to leave. I told you I had a bad feeling about this all along, but you're right. We have to find Sam and Tim."

"Yeah," John said. "I'm scared too, man. But we'll stick together. We'll find them."

The leaves crunched underfoot as they traveled deeper into the woods. The sun was directly above them, soaking through the trees and beating down on their necks. John was cursing and swatting at gnats while Patrick alternated calling for Sam and Tim.

There was no answer.

"Do you think we should split up?" Dean asked.

"No," said Patrick.

"No way," said John.

"Well, I don't know," Dean said. "I just thought we could cover more ground."

"It's not safe," Patrick said. "We're already split up."

The three of them walked for hours, calling their friends' names and having no luck. Patrick was exhausted—both physically and mentally—and had begun mumbling to himself. His hands shook.

"I think I see a clearing ahead," John called.

They ran to catch up with him. They had walked so long that the sun had begun to go down behind the tree line. Patrick stepped forward and moved some brush out of the way. Scanning the area, he saw where they had arrived.

Back at the campground.

CHAPTER FIFTEEN

"Pat?"

"Patrick?"

He could hear his friends calling his name, but it wasn't truly clicking in his mind. He stared in disbelief. His mind seemed to move in slow motion as the brutal southern heat sent waves of exhaustion through him.

"How?" was all he could manage to say.

"Man, I really don't know," John said. "I don't think we turned once the whole time we were walking."

Dean put his hand on his shoulder. "Look man, I know you don't want to hear this, but I really think we need to stop for now. If we continue looking, we're going to die out there from a heat stroke or something, and that's not helping anyone."

"Besides," John said, "It's getting dark. We already have a fire pit here, and Sam and Tim might come back here looking for us."

He was swaying from front to back.

"Patrick?" Dean said. "Hey man, I think you need some—"

Patrick took a step forward and fell flat on his face.

When Patrick woke, he heard the crackling of a fire. It was dark, and his nose felt broken.

"There he is," said John. "Damn man, I tried to catch you, but you just passed the fuck out. Your nose was bleeding pretty bad, too. How do you feel?"

"Where's Sam?"

Dean and John exchanged glances.

"Pat, we still haven't found him," Dean said. "We had to stop for the night, remember?"

"We can't stop."

"You got so hot, you almost died. We had to stop. What did you want us to do, tie you to a log and carry you?"

He sat up and put his hand to his nose. He winced in pain and drew his hand back quickly. It was definitely broken.

"I fucking hate this place," he said, holding back tears. "More than anything."

"We'll find Sam and Tim," John said. "And then we'll get the hell out of here."

Standing up, he glanced around the campground. Everything was gone, except for the fire. "I'm so hungry," he said.

Dean reached into his pocket and pulled out some individually wrapped Lifesavers candies. "This is all we have," he said.

"That's it?"

"Yeah, man. Everything was gone when we got back, remember? The tent, the car, everything."

"Well," John said. "Almost everything." He pulled a plastic sack out of his pocket. It was the weed.

"So, all we have to survive on is a few pieces of candy and something that will make me even more hungry."

"Does that mean you don't want to smoke it?"

He thought about the pain in his nose. "No," he said. "Let's do it."

Dean dug the old soda can out of the fire pit and packed it with the weed. They took turns puffing and passing. Once all the weed in the can was gone, they walked down to the creek and drank from the water on their hands and knees.

They returned to their seats at the fire and sat in silence for a while, each of them occasionally tossing more kindling into the pit. Even with the sun down, the heat of the night was almost unbearable; each of them had to move their seats back from the fire. When they sat back down, John sighed loudly. "I need to tell you guys something," he said.

"What's up?" Patrick asked.

"It's just... I feel bad for even bringing it up with Sam and Tim being missing. I mean I know there's a lot going on right now, but I'm going to explode if I don't tell someone."

"We're listening," Dean said.

John smiled weakly. "Thanks. Well, it's about Ronnie. You guys know he's been nothing but trouble for me and my mom. He's been stealing money from me and threatening to leave my mom if I told her. And she depends on him so much—financially and all—and that's why I didn't say anything for so long. But I had decided to finally put a stop to it, I mean I know he's abusive to her, and I was going to tell her about everything after this trip. I had decided that I would take on extra hours at the store, whatever I had to do to help her out. I was going to get her to leave him for good."

"Why can't you?" Dean asked.

John's chest rose and fell dramatically. He was on the verge of sobbing. "When I was getting ready to leave for the trip, I overheard them arguing. That son of a bitch got my mom pregnant, and he blamed her for it. I heard her apologizing, and he was yelling at her and calling her names. I confronted the piece of shit, and I swear I wanted to kill him." John lost control of his emotions and began to cry. Hot tears streamed down his face.

"Shit, man," Patrick said. "I'm sorry."

"Yeah," Dean said. "But that's not the worst thing ever, is it? I mean can't she just leave him and get child support or something?"

John struggled to regain control of himself. "I don't know," he said. "I just hate seeing her suffer. She deserves better, and I hate him so much. I'm afraid he'll try to kill her if she leaves. He's threatened her before."

"Fuck him," Patrick said. "You know, I could get my dad to go over there and kick his ass." All three of them burst into laughter at that. John laughed the hardest, choking back sobs.

"Thanks, guys," he said.

Dean said, "We really all have some fucked up families, don't we?"

"Yeah."

"Definitely."

John said, "We're going to find your brother, Pat. I know it."

He stood up and put some more wood into the fire. "I sure hope so," he said.

———◦———

Despite the many arguments put up by Dean and John, Patrick insisted on taking the first watch when it came time to go to sleep. He was positive he wouldn't be able to sleep even if he wanted to.

Sitting in the dark by the dying fire, he thought about their current situation and began to cry. How could he let this happen to his little brother? Sam was the one person who always had his back. And, truthfully, Patrick was likely the only person who had stood by Sam through it all. When Sam was getting tripped in the hallway, or called a faggot by everyone in the school, Patrick was always there for him, because they were brothers. The two of them were close, whether Patrick liked to admit it or not. He loved Sam, and he felt responsible for his current predicament.

Where are you Sam? What happened to you? Are you hurt?

He watched his friends as they slept, and he felt very uncomfortable. It was the lack of noise that drove him crazy. Even the creek—which usually made plenty of noise—was too quiet. The sky was too dark. He was too tired.

Too scared.

There was something else that was bothering him. That goddamned bridge. It was staring at him.

"Stop it," Patrick said under his breath. He looked away from it, but he couldn't turn his back to it. He didn't want to turn his back to anything.

When he was a small kid, he had been terrified to get off his bed at night. If he had needed to use the bathroom, or get some water, he would try his best to wait until morning. If he had stepped on the floor, he was sure that a hand would have reached out from under the bed and pulled him under where he could never come back out.

He'd had a recurring dream when he was young. He would walk into his parents' bedroom to tell them he had wet the bed, but they wouldn't be there. He heard a scratching noise from under the bed and then, like the Wicked Witch of the West coming from under the house that had killed her, a clawed, green-spotted hand would yank him under the bed. He could see his parents down the hall, looking for him and he wanted to scream for them, to tell them that he was right there, and he needed their help, but the hand was squeezing his throat, and he could only squeak hoarsely.

After those dreams, he had requested that his mattress be put directly on the floor.

At that moment, in the middle of the dark campground, with only a small flicker from the campfire, he wished that he had eyes in the back of his head because he felt that, at any moment, a green-spotted hand was just about to grab him from behind, and he wouldn't be able to call for help. A shudder ran down his spine.

A crash came from the woods behind him.

Patrick screamed.

CHAPTER SIXTEEN

Dean and John both jumped up from their sleep. "What's going on?" John asked.

Dean was covered in a cold sweat. He looked like he was going to puke.

Backing against them, Patrick could only point in the direction of the noise. It was getting louder now. Whatever was out there, it was getting closer.

"Oh my God," said Dean. "I was just dreaming about him. Always dreaming about him."

"Who?"

"The Goatman."

"Stop it with that shit," John said. "It's fucking ridiculous."

"Is it?"

It sounded like a drunk grizzly bear was running through the trees at full speed, slamming into everything in its path.

There was another noise.

Coming from the direction of the covered bridge, a voice cried out. It was impossible to tell what it was saying, but it sounded like someone in distress.

"Whatever is in the woods, it's almost here," Patrick said, his voice shaking. He turned to run, looking over his shoulder.

Dean and John followed him.

Dean said, panting, "Are we really going towards the bridge? Didn't you hear that?"

Patrick wasn't slowing down. Neither did they.

Daring one more glance over his shoulder, he saw the outline of a figure coming through the trees on the other side of the creek.

"Fuck! Fuck! Fuck! Faster!"

John looked behind them and screamed. Something was running after them at a full trot, and whatever it was, it seemed to be chasing them directly toward the bridge.

Standing in the middle of the bridge, was a small-framed person. The person was facing the open window overlooking the creek.

Patrick stepped forward a few feet. Out of breath, he called, "Sam? Is that you?"

The person turned his head and frowned.

"Hello?" he called. "Sam?"

Sam turned so that his face showed in the moonlight. Patrick rushed over and put his arms around him. Dean and John came over to them as well.

"Oh my God," he said. "Sam! You're okay! What happened to you?"

"We have to jump," Sam said.

"What?"

Sam pointed behind him. "He's not giving us any other choice."

Patrick had been so excited to find Sam that he had completely forgotten that he was being chased by something. He turned his head slowly and saw what his brother was pointing at.

In the dark it was hard to make out specific details, but there was a large man standing at the entrance to the bridge. Only, he didn't appear to be a normal man. Sticking out of the top of his head were curved horns.

Dean wailed and clung to Patrick. John reached down and picked up a rock.

"Get the fuck out of here, you creep!" John demanded. He tossed the rock and missed the figure by at least a foot.

The thing just stood there, breathing.

"We have to jump," Sam said. He climbed into the window facing the creek, and before Patrick could protest, Sam jumped into the flowing water.

Patrick hesitated for a moment—only a moment. What motivated him was the Goatman running in his direction. He could hear the heavy breathing, the animalistic noises.

He peered out of the window, and he could just barely make out Sam pulling himself out of the creek.

Okay, he made it. I can do this.

Gathering his courage, he jumped. Dean and John followed closely behind.

The Goatman bellowed in frustration after swiping for John's ankle and missing by mere inches.

He hit the cold water and instantly went numb. His mind was moving at a speed ten times faster than his body could manage. When his head came above water, he could see Sam standing on the creek bank, shivering.

Dean and John slammed into the water behind him. Dean surfaced immediately, screaming in pain. The creek water turned a crimson hue all around them.

"My leg! I sliced my leg on a rock or something. Goddamn, it hurts!"

Patrick waded to Dean, and John helped him lift Dean out of the water. Above them, the horned man-beast watched.

"Come on!" Patrick shouted. "Dean, I need you to walk!"

"I'm trying!" Dean said through gritted teeth. The blood poured from the six-inch gash in his leg.

Reaching the bank, he pulled himself from the water first, then he turned to help John drag Dean onto the bank. As soon as they were all on solid ground, Patrick glanced toward the bridge's window.

The Goatman was gone.

A *clop-clop-clop* sound echoed on the wooden floor of the bridge.

"We have to go, now," Patrick said.

Sam stood with his arms by his side, emotionless, speechless. Dean was trying not to scream. Every step he took sent a gush of blood down the side of his leg.

"We need to wrap his leg," John said. "It's really bad."

"If we stop now," Patrick said, "We're dead. Plain and simple. That crazy fucker is coming down here."

"I can walk," Dean said. "Let's just go."

He glanced around. To their right was the creek and the road out of this hell-hole. To their left were more woods. When Patrick looked back to the right again, his decision was made. The Goatman stood twenty yards away, blocking their path to the road out of the campgrounds.

"Come on," he said. "This way."

Patrick and John each put one of Dean's arms over their shoulders and helped him hop along between them. Sam followed behind.

It was very dark, and their only source of light—the small cigarette lighter—had just been soaked in the creek. Patrick had to walk with his free arm in front of him, shielding his eyes and face from the many branches and bushes in their way. He could feel things crawling on him, and he tried not to think about what they could be.

Daring a glance behind them, he saw that the creature had vanished. His heart jumped in his chest and cold sweat mixed with the creek water on his skin. "I'm so sorry I got you guys into this," he said.

Nobody offered any reprieve.

He knew they had to keep moving, but they couldn't see where they were going, and Dean needed medical attention—or, at least, the best they would be able to provide. Limbs continued to scratch their arms and faces, and Dean was moaning in pain.

John looked behind them. "I think he's left us alone," he said. "At least for now."

They entered a small clearing where the moon offered some light, and they set Dean down on the ground. Sam stared silently at the trees.

Patrick took off his socks and tied them together. "This will have to do," he said. He inspected the gash in Dean's leg. It was bad. "Look at me," he said to Dean.

Dean, tears in his eyes, looked at him. "I know what you're going to say. It's going to hurt. Just do it."

He wrapped the socks around the gash and tightened them until they were wrapped around the wound twice. Blood had already begun to soak through. Dean didn't make a sound.

"Okay," John said. "What do we do now?"

Nobody spoke.

Sam was still standing away from the group, facing the trees.

"Sam," Patrick called.

"Sam!"

Wiping his bloody hands on his shorts, he stood up. He walked over to Sam and put his hand on his shoulder.

Sam jumped.

"Sam, are you okay? You haven't said a word since the bridge."

"I don't think I am, Patrick. Not at all." He wouldn't face his brother.

"What happened to you? Where did you go? We came back, and you were just... gone."

Sam turned and faced his brother. His expression was that of someone who just met a stranger. "Came back from where?" he said.

"Sam, we went looking for Tim. We were only gone half an hour. Someone put the Suburban in the river.

When we came back to the campground, everything was gone. Including you."

"That's strange."

He was terrified by his brother's apathy and confusion.

That's strange? Who the fuck says that?

"Sam, you're freaking me out."

"I was freaked out when you left me alone."

"You volunteered."

"You're supposed to take care of me. I'm young and stupid."

Sam was not acting like himself. He was sure of that. What had happened to him out here?

"What did you see? Where did you go?"

"I saw him."

A chill went down his spine.

Sam continued, "I saw where he died. It's a tree with a rope."

"Where he died? What do you mean by that? You're not making any sense."

"He whispered it in my ear. That's how I know. I fell down when I ran."

"Ran?"

"Yes. From them."

"Sam, listen to me. You have to start making sense. I don't know what you're talking about."

Sam sighed. "It's hard to remember some of it. I hit my head. I told you."

"Try harder."

"I just know that I saw some people coming towards me, and they had weapons. Shovels, axes, stuff like that. I ran towards the bridge and I tripped and hit my head. I woke up, and the Goatman was kneeling over me. He told me that he would spare me if I showed everyone where he had died."

Okay, he thought. *Sam was on the bridge the whole fucking time. He had been knocked out when he fell and he had imagined the rest. Right?*

He didn't think so. After all, they had just been chased by the lunatic.

"Can you take us to that tree?"

"Of course. I have to."

CHAPTER SEVENTEEN

"He's not well," John said. "The bleeding hasn't stopped, and he's burning up."

Patrick and Sam knelt next to Dean.

"Dean?" Patrick said. "We can't stop moving. That thing could be headed in our direction. And we still have to find Tim."

"I know that."

"Can you walk?"

"I don't know. Maybe."

"Let me help you up."

The insects of the night cheered Dean on loudly as Patrick and John helped him back to his feet. Dean whimpered. "I sliced it up pretty damn good, didn't I?"

He glanced at Dean's blood-soaked socks. "Yeah, buddy. You did. But it should be okay."

"Easy for you to say."

They moved at a slow pace, but Dean didn't complain once, except for the occasional hiss of air through his teeth.

Sam directed them.

John said, "Tell me again where we're going?"

"I honestly don't know," Patrick said. "A tree with a noose, I guess."

"And why the fuck are we doing that?"

"I don't know," he admitted. "I guess I just thought that it might have a path leading to it that we could follow out of here or something."

"If it even exists."

"It does," Sam said.

Dean was using a makeshift crutch to help him walk. John had found a newly-fallen branch on the ground which was shaped closely enough to work, and he had accepted it graciously.

What time is it? he wondered. It was impossible to see the sky through all the trees, but even if he had been able to, he wouldn't have had a clue how to tell time by the moon and stars. It had to be at least three in the morning.

"I think this is what my cousin is always talking about when he warns me to stay away from white people," Dean said. "We got ourselves into some real white people trouble this time."

Everyone laughed.

"I'm sorry," Patrick said. "Really, I am."

"It's not your fault,We all wanted to go on this trip."

"I wonder if our parents have figured it out yet?" John said, thinking of Ronnie and his rage. "You know, that we're missing."

He let out a short bark of a laugh. "I doubt it. The fucked-up thing is that we planned this so well, they won't be looking for us for a week."

<hr />

They walked on for another half-hour, taking short breaks when they absolutely had to. Dean was getting very anxious. "Are we close?" he asked Sam.

"Yes," Sam said. "Very."

"We're going to have to stop when we get there," said Dean. "I can't do this anymore. I feel like I'm dying. So dizzy."

"It's right up here," Sam said. "Over this hill."

Coming over the hill, Patrick could see that the area was slightly open. The moonlight lit the small patch of land and, in the middle of the clearing, there was a tree.

The Hanging Tree.

Dean froze. "I... I've... I've seen this. I didn't think we'd actually find anything, but I've seen this."

"What do you mean, you've seen this?" he asked.

"In my dream. I told you... with the girls. And the snakes. This is bad. We need to leave."

"We know we need to leave," John said. "We're trying to leave. We're also trying to find our friend."

"He's gone," Dean said, his chest hitching. "I'm sorry, but he's gone. We need to go. *Now.*"

"You need to rest before you fucking die," Patrick said. "Just sit down for a while. I've got to piss. Then we can talk."

He walked away a few yards and began peeing on a log when he heard a rattling noise.

"D'you guys hear that?" he called. Finishing, he zipped his shorts and turned to join the group when he heard the noise again. It seemed to be coming from the log.

"Patrick, get away from there!" Dean screamed.

He turned around and looked at the log. A swarm of pissed-off snakes, wet with urine, raced towards him. Screaming in terror, he bolted in the opposite direction. One of the snakes lunged at him. Its fangs sank into the fabric of his shorts, just missing his skin.

John had taken off his shirt and was clicking the lighter and cursing, "Light, you motherfucker!" Finally, the lighter produced a flame, and John's shirt—dry by now, had been for an hour or more—caught fire. As Patrick raced past him, John waved the flaming end of his shirt. The snake leading the chase struck at the flame but quickly retreated after feeling the heat on its face.

Soon, all the serpents had disappeared.

CHAPTER EIGHTEEN

arefully, the group gathered enough wood and leaves to start a small fire, mostly for the light it would provide, but also because it would keep away most predators. Although it was very warm outside, and they were huddled around the flames, they still shivered.

"Snakes don't chase people," Dean said.

Patrick hadn't spoken much since the incident. He felt stupid, really. There had to be an old saying somewhere about pissing on a snake nest and how you shouldn't do it. He felt the back of his shorts where the snake had nearly bit him. There were two punctures in the material. His blood turned to ice.

"I'm telling you," Dean said. "This place is pure evil. We could be sitting on top of a portal to Hell or something."

Sam spoke up. "That tree is where they hanged him. He told me. The village people made him this way."

"That's horseshit," John said. "I don't believe he told you anything."

"It's not horseshit," Dean said. "I read about this online. There was a man. I think he was a goat farmer or something. He got chased out of his home because he was black, and the locals didn't like him. They hanged him, and then they found his house and killed his family."

"So, we're believing he's a ghost then?" Patrick asked. "A demon?"

The fire was causing their shadows to dance on the trees around them. The only sound was the crackling of the fire.

"Whatever he is," Dean said. "We've seen him. You can't deny that. He chased us."

"I'm so hungry," Sam said, in his small voice.

"I think we all are," Patrick responded.

"There's something else," Dean continued. "I read that the locals know about this noose hanging here. They say that, no matter how many times it gets taken down, it's back again the next day."

John stood up. "Let's pull the fucker down then. At this point, I'm ready to sit here and watch it. Don't have much else to do, do I?"

Patrick thought about what John said. He thought about what Sam had said. The Goatman had supposedly wanted Sam to take the rest of them to this place. But why hadn't the Goatman hurt Sam? He'd had every opportunity.

"What if he really is a ghost?" Patrick said.

John sighed loudly.

"I'm serious," he continued. "If he told Sam to take us here, and this is where he was hanged, maybe we're supposed to do something. You know, to set his spirit free or something."

"Like what?"

He thought for a moment. But it was Sam who spoke up. "Let's burn the noose down," he said.

Patrick said, "Let's burn the whole goddamned tree down."

<hr>

Sam approached the tree first. It was a massive old oak tree with hollow places all throughout the trunk. Apprehensive, he placed his hands on the wood. "Are you sure about this?" he asked his brother.

"Why not?"

Sam stepped back from the tree. "I don't know," he said. "I just have a strange feeling."

"Everything out here gives me a strange feeling," John said. "I'm for it. Thing gives me the creeps. Dean?"

Dean was sitting on the ground, nursing his leg. "I was thinking. Maybe the fire will act as a beacon. For Tim."

Patrick hadn't thought about that. What if the blaze attracts something or someone else?

They could move on if that happened, he figured. They could get attacked here with or without a fire, anyways.

"I say we do it," he said. "I don't know why, but I think we should."

"Better get to burning, then," Dean said.

Patrick nodded to John. "You have the lighter. Let's do this."

John inspected the tree. There was a good-sized pile of leaves around the base. That would be plenty to get it going, he thought. But, when he approached the tree, he decided to light the noose on fire first. Clicking the small lighter, he brought the flame to the bottom of the rope and held it underneath it.

The lighter went out.

John clicked the lighter again and held it to the rope.

The lighter went out again.

"What the hell?" he said, frustrated.

John tried to light the rope three more times, and each time, the flame extinguished on its own.

"Try lighting the leaves around the base," Patrick said.

John lit a small pile of leaves around the base of the tree with no problem. The flames jumped around quickly on the dry tinder. Sam and Patrick helped him fan the flames, and within a few minutes, the bark on the tree had caught fire.

John went around the base of the tree, lighting the dry leaves and even catching the dead vines that were wrapped around the base of the tree on fire. It was a slow process, but in a matter of minutes, the entire base of the tree was crawling in flames. Dean laughed and cheered. "Smokey the Bear is going to be pissed," he said.

"Only you would think that joke is funny," Patrick said in his best cartoon bear voice.

"Patrick," Sam said. "Who is that?"

Sam pointed. There was a young girl standing on the other side of the tree, staring at them through the flames.

"Hello?" Patrick called.

The girl stood there, staring. She had the same entranced look Sam had when he had found him on the bridge.

"Hey," Sam said. "It's okay, you can come here."

John backed up a few steps until he was close to Dean.

The girl started edging her way around the blaze.

"It's okay," Patrick said. "Are you lost?"

The girl looked to be about nine or ten. She wore a tattered old sundress the color of a wilting red rose.

"What's your name?"

"I'm Luna." She stood in front of them, arms at her sides.

"Are you lost?" he repeated.

"No."

Sam looked at him apprehensively.

"Okay," Patrick said. "Where did you come from?"

"My house." The girl pointed in the direction she had come from. "It's just over there. Are *you* lost?"

He felt sick. The girl's blank expression made him uneasy.

"Yes," Sam said. "We're lost. Do you have a phone?"

"Why are you burning the tree?"

The boys were silent.

"Why?" the girl asked again.

"We're trying to help someone," Sam said.

"You need to come with me now."

"Are you going to take us to a phone?" Patrick said.

"Was there another one of you?" The girl asked.

"Yes! Have you seen him?"

"Come with me," the girl said.

CHAPTER NINETEEN

It still hasn't been explained to me how a teenage boy from another state could do my job better than myself. I don't know if I believe in anything even remotely supernatural, but I do feel like that's my stubborn side showing. If you knew what I knew, you'd call me an ignorant bastard.

I feel like these talk show folks expect me to say something deeply profound about life and death. They figure this old man has seen enough to have an opinion about the mysteries of life. Well, I can tell you this: everything doesn't happen for a reason. If that flies in the face of all you've been told, well, I apologize for that, but I wouldn't be doing you any favors by lyin' to you.

Sometimes—a lot of times—there is absolutely no rhyme nor reason to a situation. You hear about babies being born with incurable diseases, damned from conception, and there's always some loon to say how it's all God's plan.

God doesn't have a plan for you.

Just ask them boys I found in the woods twelve years ago.

Elmer Davis shot up in his hospital bed and gasped for air. Tiny plastic tubes protruded from his nose, his arms, his crotch.

Uncomfortable was the understatement of the century.

His vision was blurry and he felt nauseous. Slowly, his sight began to return, and Elmer saw his IV drip. Moving on to the table on the far side of the room, he saw flowers, food, and cards.

When he turned his head to the other side of the room, he gasped. There was an old man sitting in a chair, watching him.

Elmer closed his eyes, opened them, blinked, and the man was still sitting there. Staring.

"Who are you?"

The old man straightened his back until it made a loud cracking sound, sighed, and sat forward in his chair. "My name isn't important."

Elmer pulled the breathing tubes out of his nose and small drops of blood leaked out, staining the hospital sheets.

"That's normal," the old man said.

"What is going on?"

"You tried to warn the boys, yes?"

Elmer's eyes narrowed. He was trying to piece together the moments that had led to his arrival in this hospital bed. "What boys?" he said. But he knew.

The old man smiled. "I know it's probably not the most ideal situation for you. I understand, trust me when I say that. But you are really their only hope."

"What can I do?"

"You'll know," said the old man. "And don't beat yourself up if you can't fix it. You can't fix everything all the time. But you do need to go. Now."

The lights in the hospital went out abruptly, and there were screams coming from all directions down the hall. Elmer was shaking and weak. He began pulling all the tubes and wires off—and out of—his body, wincing and gasping in pain.

A few moments later, the power returned, but the lights kept flickering. The weather outside was ramping up to a violent storm, the winds howling and thunder booming. Outside his room, Elmer could see nurses rushing past, yelling to each other. Elmer's nose was bleeding even harder now.

Elmer looked to the chair where the old man had sat. The old man was gone.

There was a pile of clothes at the end of the hospital bed. A pair of blue jeans, a Linkin Park T-shirt, a hat, and a pair of Converse shoes. Hurriedly, Elmer put the clothes on and stumbled into the hall.

The panic had not died down, and Elmer could hear nurses shouting about the generator. Elmer heard the word tornado a few times, and a woman was standing down the hall screaming about her husband's blood pressure pills.

Quickly, he worked his way down the hall, looking for the staircase. A couple of nurses glanced at him like they recognized him, but they kept going in the other direction, preoccupied with the confusion. Soon, Elmer found the stairwell and descended the staircase.

Reaching the ground floor of the hospital, Elmer saw his mother in the café, sitting alone and eating a sandwich. He wanted to walk in there, to tell her he was okay, but he couldn't. He had something to do.

In the upper deck of the parking lot, Elmer stood, scanning the vehicles. His Jeep was probably still at the school, he figured. He would need to find his mom's Honda. The rain was coming down in sheets and lightning raced across the sky. A shout came from behind him. One of the nurses.

"Hey! Stop! You aren't fit to leave!"

Without turning around, he broke into a run down the center of the parking lot.

"Where the hell is security?" he heard the charge nurse say in frustration.

He was getting soaked. Thunder shook the parking deck, and several of the car alarms began screaming. Water ran in small rivers to the drains in the corners of the parking deck, but Elmer's shoes had already become soaked through.

Where is the damn car?

A bolt of lightning struck a tree a quarter-mile away, and the light illuminated the entire area for a moment. Elmer saw the Honda, a red Civic, one row over. Security had made it outside and was calling after him. Elmer's heart was racing.

He reached the car and began fumbling underneath the frame for the magnetic hide-a-key. His fingers closed around the small box, and he pulled it free. His hands shaking, he looked up and saw a guard with a flashlight three vehicles away. The box slipped out of his fingers and fell to the ground, the river of water carrying it away.

"Shit!" Elmer yelled. He was sure they would catch him and haul him back to his hospital bed. He couldn't let that happen.

In a panic, he fished around in the dark for the box, nabbing it just before it could swirl down the storm drain.

"Stop, kid! What do you think you're doing?"

Elmer pulled the key out of the box and let the box drop to the ground. He unlocked the car, and jumped in the driver's seat, closing and locking the door just before the guard could grab him.

The guard tapped on the window.

"You need to think about what you're doing!" he shouted.

Elmer started the car and turned on the headlights.

The guard stood back. He pulled out his radio and shouted something into it.

Backing the car out of the spot, Elmer left the hospital parking garage.

CHAPTER TWENTY

The girl from the woods assured the boys that her house wasn't far. She didn't say much else. Patrick and John helped Dean walk, since his leg seemed to be getting worse rather than better.

Sam was trying his hardest to get the girl to say, well, anything. He wasn't having any luck. The most he had gotten out of her was a shrug.

Then he struck a nerve.

"What can you tell us about the Goatman?" he asked her. She stopped walking.

"We don't talk about him," she said. "Never."

Sam looked at her for a moment, wondering what to say next. Patrick spoke for him.

"How much further? Dean needs help, he's still bleeding."

"We're here."

The girl pushed aside the bushes and began descending some wood planks that had been crudely placed into the side of a small hill. At the end of the steps was an old wooden cabin that reminded him of *Snow White and the Seven Dwarves*.

An old man sat in a creaky rocking chair on the porch, smoking a cigarette. He wore denim suspenders over a red and black checkered flannel shirt. His glasses covered most of his face, and their frames were so dirty, they looked yellow.

"Luna," he barked. "Where you been girl? Ma is worried sick!"

"I got some lost people with me, Grandpa. Can't you see 'em?"

The old man took off his glasses and rubbed them on his dirty clothes. He spat on the floor of the porch. "I can't see shit, girl. You know that."

"Well they're right there!" She pointed at the group of them.

"Hello, sir." Patrick said. "We're so glad... Luna found us. We were lost out there, and we really need to use—"

"How many are ya?" Grandpa said.

"Sir?"

"How many of you are there?"

He looked around. "Well," he said. "There's four of us here, including myself. And there was—"

"Another one, I know."

"Is he here?"

"Yeah. He's here. Boy was lost as a run-over dog. But he's inside." Grandpa spat again. "Reckon we'll have you for dinner. I know you're hungry."

"We sure are," Sam said.

"Really, I think what's most important is the phone," Patrick said. "Dean here, he cut his leg pretty bad, and I think it's infected."

"I'll get my son to look at the cut," Grandpa said. "He's a bit of a medical expert. But you boys will eat. I won't take no."

<hr>

The interior of the cabin looked about as drab as the exterior, and there was a dank aroma in the air that reminded him of the day his Biology class had dissected baby sharks. Grandpa followed the boys in at a snail's pace, taking the rear.

"Ma!" he shouted in his croaky voice. "Get some food goin'! We got more company. Friends of the other boy!"

Dean found a chair and sat down, holding his leg at an awkward angle. He hissed in air every time he moved it.

Grandpa looked at Dean's leg. "Shame," he said, before walking through the doorway into the adjoining room.

"Shame?" Dean said under his breath. "What the fuck does that mean?"

"I don't know," Patrick said. "I think he's probably senile or some—"

"Don't talk about Grandpa like that." Luna was standing in the doorway, listening to their conversation.

"Oh, no," John said. "They were just—"

"Heard 'em."

Dean looked at Luna. "Where is the phone? We really need to make a call."

Luna looked at Dean, then at Patrick, John, and Sam, turning her head slowly between each one.

"A phone?" Patrick asked. "You said you had one?"

Luna turned around and ran out of the room.

The sound of feet shuffling came from the other side of the house. A shambling shell of an old woman came creeping through the doorway Grandpa had left through. He thought she looked like the woman from that old painting of the couple in front of the farmhouse. All she needed was a pitchfork.

Without looking up from the floor, the woman said, "Sit." Patrick and the rest of them found places at the table in front of them. The old woman walked out of the room and began making noise in the kitchen.

"Where the hell is Tim?" John said.

"I don't know," said Patrick. "And it seems like these people are allergic to questions."

Sam was sitting next to him, shaking. "Guys," he said. "Do you think us burning that tree did anything to stop it?"

"Stop what?" Patrick said.

"The evil in these woods."

CHAPTER TWENTY-ONE

Elmer wanted to stop by his house and get his phone, but he knew he didn't have time. He was already almost too late. The coma was working against him. He didn't know how he knew the things he did, or why. He just knew that sometimes he knew things. And sometimes he could stop bad things from happening with that knowledge. Right now, he knew that he had to find Sheriff Paul Stanton in Blakely, Georgia.

The storm seemed to ease up the further he got from the hospital. Elmer felt terrible for stealing his mom's car, but she would understand...maybe. She had certainly seen him do strange, unexplainable things before. He was thankful that the tank was nearly full because he didn't even have a single dollar with him. There were a few quarters in the cup holder, though.

Elmer pulled into a gas station in Columbia, Alabama, just a couple of miles from the Alabama-Georgia border. Starving, he gathered the quarters and entered. The man behind the counter looked up from his paper but didn't speak. Elmer counted his money. A dollar seventy-five. He walked to the counter.

"Sir," he said. "What can I get to eat for this? And can I maybe get a styrofoam cup or something like that for some water?"

The man eyed the quarters on the counter.

"Are you okay, kid? You look like boiled shit."

"I'm just hungry."

The man set down the newspaper. "Keep your money," he said, reaching under the counter. "I got half a pizza here. You can have it. Was gonna give it to my dog anyway. Go get you a drink though."

Elmer thanked the man. He walked to the cooler and grabbed a Monster energy drink.

"That kinda night?" the clerk said.

"You're damn right."

The old woman—Ma—returned from the kitchen after a few minutes with a large pot. Steam rolled over the sides, emitting a foul, warm stench not unlike a dead skunk cooking on the side of the road .

"Pa! Pa! It's time to eat!" She set the pot down and wiped her nose with the back of her hand and snorted, causing a lumpy, dark, cancerous knot on her neck to jiggle.

Patrick gagged silently.

Luna walked into the kitchen, quiet as a mouse. She had bowls and spoons with her. Going around the table, she gave one of each to the boys and they thanked her but were not welcomed back.

Grandpa walked into the dining room, his thumbs tight beneath his suspenders, and sat at the far end of the table. He rubbed his red nose and sat in silence as he looked across each of the boys. "Hope you boys are hungry." His words were dry and unpleasant. "Ma put a lot of effort into this meal."

"Yes, sir," Patrick said. "Thank you."

"Luna," Pa said. "Go get your brother."

Luna grinned and walked out of the room.

"Where's Tim?" John asked.

"Your other friend?" Pa said flatly, making no eye contact. "He's not hungry."

Dean shifted in his chair and let out a moan. His arm was starting to shake.

Luna returned to the dining room and rubbed her tongue against the front of her teeth. A large man in a once-white shirt followed her. He was so tall he had to duck when he walked through the door frame.

"This here is Jeb," Pa said. "Say hi, Jeb. We got company."

"Hi." Jeb's mouth hung loose as he exhaled loudly, his brow tight as he scowled at them.

"Jeb, here, is our little gifted one. He's a regular doc, he is. He'll take a look at your leg after dinner." Pa tipped a steak knife at Dean's leg.

"Th-thanks," Dean said, and his tongue came out to lick his lips. His right hand was still shaking, the pain was clearly getting to be too much.

Ma walked around the table, her heavy hips swaying as she dumped the dark, soupy substance into everyone's bowl. The boys thanked her. The stench climbed from the liquid and into their noses, clawing down their throats. They passed glances to one another and, in silent agreement, they all knew not to complain. Ma dumped the soup into her own bowl last before sitting down in her seat.

The room was dim and damp. The yellowed wallpaper was peeling at the corners and turning brown with rot. Candles provided the only light, making it hard to see anything with any real clarity. Patrick exchanged uncomfortable glances with the rest of the group, some of them too afraid to even look up from the soup.

Grandpa stood up at the end of the table, reaching up to scratch at his curly gray chest hair peeking out from his undershirt. "Time we say grace. We need to be thankful for everything we're given." His voice came at a crawl, one scratched from years of tobacco use. "Ma, do you want the honors?"

"Yeah, Pa. I'll do it. Now sit down 'fore you fall down." Pa sat down, grumbling.

Ma bowed her head. "Thank you, oh Great One for all you've given us. The protection we've been allowed.

The food you've provided. Help us to continue to serve in your honor."

"Amen," Pa said, his head slowly rising from a bow. "Now let's eat."

Patrick didn't feel like eating at all, his stomach told him he'd sooner eat his shoe than that soup. He moved the slop around in the bowl, trying to see what actually was in it, but it was too dark in the room to tell and each time it moved the smell seemed to come again fresh, as if it had grown pointed legs and scaled down his nostrils.

Sam was making a face at him which said that he felt the same. He noticed that Dean and John were picking at their food also.

"There something wrong?" Jeb asked through a mouthful of soup, a brown string of it leaking down the corner of his wrinkled mouth.

"Oh," Patrick said. "I'm just not very hungry. This trip has my stomach all in knots, you know? I'd really love to make that phone call." Beneath the table he wrung his hands together.

Jeb slammed his spoon on the table so hard that one of the candles fell on its side, the flame went out and a small smoky trail sizzled.

Pa stared at him for a moment, then licked his spoon clean and pointed it at him. "Are you trying to hurt Ma's feelings? She made this meal out of the kindness of her heart! A lot of sacrifice goes into every meal around here. Have you ever thought about that? Have you ever thought about what it means to not be wasteful? No. You don't give a damn, do you? You're probably used to sitting on your mommy's couch, eating Cheetos out of a bag, licking your slimy little fucking fingers like the piggies you are."

Patrick sunk down into his seat. His heart slammed in his chest, and he didn't have a clue what to say next. He felt his intestines start to turn like he could shit his pants right here and right now. If he could have picked up the spoon and started eating to stop the man from talking he would have, but his hand wouldn't move.

John had both his hands on the arms of the chair, already half standing with a forced smile on his face as he spoke. "We'd really just like to get our friend and call for help. That's all. We're sorry if we come off as rude. We're just worried for our friend. And Dean's leg is—"

"Which one of you is Dean?" Jeb said, standing up and pushing his chair back in a jerky simultaneous motion that sent it clattering toward the ground and made them all jump.

"I am," Dean said. His hand was shaking so badly that his spoon clacked against his bowl.

"Tell ya what," Jeb said. "I'll take a look at that leg. Right now. Ease your mind a bit."

"You'd do that? Thanks. It hurts pretty bad. I scraped it on a ro—"

"Yeah, yeah. Let's see it." He grinned, showing a mouthful of rotted teeth.

Dean reluctantly stood up and lifted his leg until it was resting on the edge of his chair. Jeb walked over and placed a candle on the corner of the table, dust danced within the light.

"Set it up there," Jeb said, and pointed a thick finger down at the table.

Dean did as he was asked.

Jeb looked at it for a moment, slowly nodding his heavy brow as if he was looking for just the right piece of the puzzle. Then he held up his large hands and clenched his fists together, his fingers all popping at once.

Dean's lips puckered. "...wait."

Jeb wrapped his fingers around the bloody place on Dean's leg. He started twisting it from right to left, and it immediately started to crack, the sound of celery snapping and crunching.

In pure shock, it was several seconds before Dean let out a wail that filled the house and made the other boys cover their ears.

They should have run. They should have thrown the table, or hurled their bowls or grabbed their chairs, but no one moved, frozen and eyes wide.

They only watched.

"Hmm," Jeb said, and rubbed a thick and bloody finger beneath his chin. "I see the problem, and it's not good. Hold on just a second. I've got just the thing."

Jeb walked over to a drawer and pulled it open. A metallic clang echoed throughout the dining room.

"What's that?" Dean said in a nervous voice, sweat pouring down his face now.

"It's just one of my instruments," Jeb croaked, rubbing his throat. "Now let me get a closer look. You may want to bite down on something. I've really gotta prod in there."

Dean closed his eyes.

Ma seemed unconcerned with what was happening, she turned toward a mirror that was close to her seat and began to adjust her hair, trying to keep it propped around a thin balding spot around the top of her head.

Patrick saw what was in Jeb's hand, and he screamed. It was too late. Jeb brought a meat cleaver down on Dean's leg with so much force that the bone broke just below the knee. A clean, smooth cut that could have only come from a butcher's precision and years of practice. Blood sprayed in all directions, and Dean bucked like a pissed-off bull with its balls strapped up tight.

"Hold still!" Jeb screamed into Dean's face. "I'm not finished!"

The meat cleaver came down again. Patrick, John, and Sam were screaming. They stood up and backed away from the table, but the weakness in their knees held them like chains from moving any further.

Luna was underneath the table, she stuck her head out long enough to dip her spoon into Sam's bowl and take a taste, grinning at one of the boys when they caught her and frowning when they didn't grin back.

Tendons, bone, and blood flew across the room, slinging off the cleaver and hitting the walls to match the other rotten stains against the wallpaper. Jeb grabbed the leg by the foot and wiggled until it snapped off at the cut. Dean had vomited all over himself.

"There." Jeb blinked hard and then slammed the chunk of meat onto the table, rattling the bowls with the impact. "I fixed your goddamn leg. Now shut up and eat."

CHAPTER TWENTY-TWO

Ronnie Garland sat in his La-Z-Boy recliner watching *SportsCenter*. The pile of empty beer cans on the end table was impressive. He had been drinking more than usual lately, after the unfortunate news about John's mother being pregnant with his child. She was so fucking stupid for allowing that to happen. The *ESPN* hosts were talking about how the Braves were making bad decisions. Again.

"What's new?" Ronnie said. He puffed his cigar. That was his other new thing. Smoking in the house.

The phone rang. Ronnie jumped and looked at the clock on the wall. "If this is one of your stupid fuckin' friends! Calling this late." Ronnie slurred his words. He had temporarily forgotten that John wasn't even there.

Ronnie walked over to the cordless phone and picked it up, saying, "Do you know what time it is?"

"Is this John Queen's father?"

"Who's asking?"

"I'm sorry. This is hard for me to say. My name is Brother Jeff. I'm with the church."

"Yeah? I'm his step-dad. What did he do wrong now?"

"Sir. I was going through some paperwork when I saw that your wife had paid for John's trip. I also have slips for Patrick and Sam Hall, Dean Fredrick, and Tim Johnson."

"Get to the point, Brother..."

"Jeff, yes... Well, none of those boys are with us. I was just calling all the parents to let them know. In case they didn't already, of course. I'm sorry it took us so long to—"

"What do you mean they're not with you?"

"I mean, they never got on the bus."

Ronnie hung up the phone.

John's mother walked into the room in her nightgown. "What's going on?"

Ronnie, breathing heavily and using the wall for support, said, "Can we find out where John's phone is from the phone company?"

"Yeah," she said. "But why? What is it?"

"I'm gonna kill that little shit. I told you he wasn't the angel you thought he was. Him and his friends played hooky on their little church trip. That's fine. When I find him, he won't sit down for the rest of the summer."

"What are you going to do, Ronnie? You've been drinking, you can't just—"

Ronnie closed the gap between himself and John's mother in a matter of seconds. Using the back of his hand, he knocked her to the floor. She cried out in pain. Ronnie grabbed her by the hair and yanked her head back so that she was looking him in the eye. "I can't what?" he said.

Bleeding, crying, and convulsing, Dean was forced to finish his meal while the others watched. At one point, when he gagged and turned to puke, he was told that his friends would have to eat it if he did.

Patrick had a black eye. He had been headbutted by Jeb when he tried to protest Dean's amputation. Sam was hysterical, trying his best not to lose it.

"You see," Grandpa said. "You boys do know how to have a nice quiet dinner. That's a good quality to have, just knowing when to shut the fuck up. Of course, some don't have that quality about them automatically. They have to be taught, and hey, that's okay, too."

Dean's hand was shaking so badly that his soup was splattering the table.

"Every last bit, boy. I told you. We don't waste 'round here." Jeb said. "And that goes for the rest of you too! It's almost like you don't want any dessert!"

Patrick thought that the last thing he wanted was any kind of food these people had to offer. Grudgingly, he finished his meal with the rest of them.

Grandpa stood up and surveyed the room. "Jeb, you've really made a mess, boy."

"Yes, sir," Jeb said. "Hope it didn't ruin your appetite."

They both laughed.

———⸙———

Elmer arrived at the Early County Sheriff's office in the dead of night. The violent, ugly weather seemed to have followed him. Sitting in the car, Elmer's hands were shaking. He knew what was coming, and he knew what had already happened. That was how things always were for Elmer, and nobody ever believed him... except for a strange old man in a hospital room.

Elmer watched the wiper blades dodge tediously from left to right and back to left. There, beyond the windshield, was a man in the building, sitting at a desk. He took a deep breath and turned off the ignition.

Elmer had parked directly in front of the small building, but he still managed to get soaked on the way to the front door. A small bell chimed to announce his entrance.

Clearly startled, the deputy set down his magazine and removed his feet from the top of his desk. "C-can I help you, son?" He stood up, straightening his uniform.

"I need to speak with the Sheriff. It's an emergency." The rain came down harder.

"Well, now. Sheriff Stanton is out right at the moment. What can I do for ya? Name's Deputy Benny Dumear." He held out his hand.

"I'm sorry, sir," Elmer said. "But this isn't your burden. Sheriff Stanton needs to hear what I have to say."

Benny began to protest but when he saw the headlights approaching outside, he realized that the sheriff had returned. "You got your wish, kid." He ambled over to the coffee maker and turned it on

The door chimed again and in walked a rugged man, an old-school type of sheriff, spurs and the like.

"Kid's here to see you, Paul. I wasn't good enough," Benny said, pouring himself a cup of coffee.

The sheriff glanced at Elmer. "Damn, you're tall. You play basketball?"

"No, sir."

"Shame. You might wanna think about it. Could be a real opportunity. I mean, if I was in your shoes—"

"Sir. People are going to die."

Stanton patted the chair across from his desk. "All right, you've got my attention."

CHAPTER TWENTY-THREE

I really hate the term "preachy" to describe me, or anything I say or stand for. I didn't pick this life or these circumstances. Trust me when I tell you that I am the last person who would ever be expected to change his ways. But things happen to people. Sometimes, there just isn't a reason for violence. It's something I live with, thinking about human nature. Thinking about my Southern Baptist upbringing. I sit down with nothing but my thoughts, and I think, are we all created equal, really? Because I don't know how that works. What does it mean to be created equal when you have babies born without eyesight or children who get cancer?

I think what I'm saying, is that something wasn't right with those folks out in those woods. And I just can't comprehend how it could go on for so long. I can't accept it. Those people out there, they were created equal to you and me, right? Were they really all playing with a full deck? What is it about that thought that bugs me so much, that I'm supposed to believe that I am capable of such heinous crimes as a human being, while still being considered "above" other animals?

―――――◦◦◦―――――

The rain dripped and trickled down through the roof of the hellish shack in the woods. Dean had turned a cold shade of blue, and Patrick, John, and Sam were having their own panic attacks.

"You know what," Jeb said. "I'm just gonna say it, Pa. I don't think these boys deserve any dessert. That ain't how I was raised, getting awarded for being an asshole."

Pa slammed his fists on the table and let out a croaky laugh. "No, Jeb. I don't reckon they do deserve anything sweet. Take 'em to the storage area. Any of 'em tries anything stupid, kill 'em. I think they know you're serious though." He eyed Dean's leg.

Dean's leg.

It lay there on the table, blood still spurting from the stump onto the vomit-covered surface.

"Alright, boys. You heard Pa. Getcha asses up now, let's go!" Jeb said, wiping his nose on his stained sleeve.

Stumbling, Patrick, Sam, and John got to their feet. Dean was hunched over the table, unmoving. "I'm not going anywhere," he said.

Jeb came across the room so fast that Sam let out a small gasp. Grabbing Dean by the back of the neck, he yanked his head up and stared into the boy's eyes. "What did you say, nigger?"

Defiant, Dean looked at Jeb. The blood draining from his face, the way his body was cold and shaking, Dean didn't feel human. There were so many things going through his mind at that point, and as his friends all stood around and watched the exchange, completely powerless, Dean knew they were the best people he'd ever met.

Dean, considering Jeb's hard face, he said, "I said, fuck you, I won't do what you tell me."

Jeb took a step back. Turning, he eyed Grandpa, who still sat in his large chair on the other side of the room. "They don't always cooperate, Jeb. You know that. Don't take it so hard. But I told you what had to be done."

"No!" Patrick said. "Dean, listen... Dean. Just come with us, we'll help you up, come on."

Dean didn't reply for a moment. A tear trickled down his face. "I can't do it, Patrick. I won't. Don't you see what's going on? We fucked up coming out here. I'm sorry, but I won't give them the satisfaction."

Jeb stepped toward Dean slowly, seeming to size him up. "It's unfortunate that you don't want to comply," he said. "Because Pa means what he says when he tells me to do something."

"Dean, come on!" shouted John.

"Shut up!" Jeb snarled. "It's too late for him. And if any of you try to interfere, you'll be next."

Dean looked up at the mountain of a man with defiance, but he didn't move.

Jeb closed his hands around the boy's throat and slammed him into the kitchen wall. His friends screamed, and Patrick—ignoring the warning—bolted across the room in an attempt to claw the man off Dean, but Jeb backhanded him so hard that he collapsed onto the floor.

Dean's eyes were bulging in his head. His remaining leg kicked in the air a foot above the ground.

"That's right," Jeb said. "Try to kick, little piggy. Try to fight it."

Dean's arms flailed wildly but he couldn't seem to fight back. John pulled Patrick up and thought, *We could just leave right now. We could just run out the door and keep running forever.*

But they didn't run. They wanted to help their friend but were unable to do a thing. Frozen in fear, they heard Dean's windpipe get crushed.

"I gotta say, kid, whoever put you up to this must really hate me," Stanton said as Elmer Davis finished his story.

The storm outside had calmed, and Elmer sat staring out the window in silence. He watched the rain roll down the glass before answering, "I don't know what you mean, sir."

"Yeah," he said. "'Course. No, it's not the first time someone has tried to tell me some stories about the Goatman, in case you were wondering. It's not funny, kid. But I have to give it to you, you've got balls coming in here like you did. Most people just call."

Elmer sat forward in his chair. "What is the Goatman?"

"Listen—"

"No, you listen. I don't know what you think I'm talking about, or what kind of game you think this is, but I'm not making up lies here. And I'm not going to have you blow me off."

Stanton crossed his hands and pursed his lips.

The phone rang, and Benny answered it.

He looked down at his desk. There was the notepad he had taken when he talked to Floyd at the gas station. "Could you give me a description of the kids?" he asked Elmer.

"I told you their names. I know what they look like."

"Well?"

"There's five of them. Three white guys, average build. One is half-black, half-Asian. All about my age. There's also a younger one; he's white too."

He looked down at his notepad again. *Five? Floyd had only mentioned four kids. Sure, he had said one was mixed, but he had only mentioned four.* He looked at Elmer. "Okay," he said. "Well, tell me what you suggest I do."

CHAPTER TWENTY-FOUR

After watching Dean's lifeless body drop to the floor, they were herded down into the cellar where the door was locked with a chain. Patrick, John, and Sam stood motionless.

"We just watched our friend die," John said, the words were cold in his mouth.

Sam was crying.

"Yeah," Patrick said. "We did." The shock gripped him like an anaconda squeezing the life out of a rodent. He found it hard to breathe.

"We're going to die," Sam said.

"No," Patrick said, finding his breath. "No, we have to find a way out. We're smarter than they are."

"Are we?" John asked. "Because we just stood and watched our best friend get murdered. We didn't even try..." He broke off in tears.

"We did try. You know it," he said.

He began feeling his way around in the dark. The floor was dirt; there were no tools or weapons hanging on the walls, nothing of any use to them anywhere. He walked up the stairs to the cellar door. He shook it, but it wouldn't budge. The chains rattled. He sat down on the cellar floor next to his brother and tried to think.

Benny got off the phone and told Stanton that he was heading to check on an accident scene.

"Who called it in?" Stanton asked.

"Some guy said he thought he saw a car behind him spin out of control. Says he wasn't really sure 'cause it was raining so hard. That's why he didn't stop, he says."

Stanton let out a small sarcastic laugh, "Let me know if you need me."

The deputy nodded and walked out into the rain.

Turning the sheriff's attention back to the problem, Elmer said, "What I'd suggest you do is go find these kids before they're all dead."

Stanton sighed and stood up from his desk. Walking to the coffee-maker, he asked, "Do you want something to drink?"

Elmer was furious. "No, I would not like something to drink. What do I have to do to get you to listen to me?"

"Calm your horses, kid. I'm getting something for the road. And you're coming with me. We're going to go catch the boogeyman."

———◆———

Deputy Benny Dumear turned on the radio in his cruiser as he was leaving the station. Sighing, he put the car in reverse. Accidents were becoming increasingly frequent in the area, and he was usually the one who had to work them. He didn't even ask anymore. But tonight, he didn't mind it so much. He'd rather be out doing something than sitting at the station and listening to some lunatic kid ramble on.

The town was dead at this hour, not that it was ever what you could call alive and jumping, but his drive was a short one with the lack of traffic. The windshield wiper blades worked furiously, but the visibility was still poor. With one hand on the wheel, he reached into the glove compartment and pulled out his secret pack of Marlboro reds. If his wife, Melissa, ever discovered that he had been smoking again, she'd kill him. He'd like to think that the job put so much stress on him that he deserved a little break, but he knew she was right. Even so, he lit the cigarette and inhaled.

The cruiser breached a hill, and Benny saw tail lights through the sheet of water on his windshield. Flicking the headlight beams to high, he slowed the car and peered out through the glass. A blue Pontiac Sunbird sat in the ditch. A sign reading *Speed Limit 40* had been knocked almost completely over, bent at its base where the car had struck it.

He parked his car on the other side of the sign and turned on his flashers. Opening his door, he threw his cigarette into the ditch and stepped out. The rain pelted his clothes and water ran in a stream from the brim of his hat. He pulled his flashlight from its holster and shined it at the car.

"Hello?" he called. "Is anyone hurt?"

———◆——

Stanton let Elmer sit in the front with him. He was starting to think the kid might not be lying to him. That didn't mean he wasn't a loony, but he was pretty sure Elmer at least believed what he was saying was true.

"So," he said, "where to?"

Elmer shifted in his seat. "I don't know," he said, looking at the floorboard. "The woods. They're in the woods somewhere."

"Well that sure narrows it down."

Elmer reached for the door handle. "You know what? I can go find someone else who actually wants to do the right thing. I don't have to listen to you belittle me. This isn't funny."

"Okay, okay, I know where the campground is. We'll start there."

"Thank you."

"I said, is there anyone there?" Benny called again as he approached the Sunbird. The engine was dead, but the car still had power. The cool rain fell hard on the sweltering ground, and steam billowed around the vehicle. He shined the flashlight into the backseat. There was some blood spatter—not a lot, just a drop here and there.

He called out again, "I'm here to help you."

Please let it not be too bad, he prayed. He'd seen too many gruesome scenes, and his stomach wasn't feeling exactly fantastic.

Rain had begun to pool in his shoes, soaking his socks miserably. A bird could have taken a bath in the brim of his hat. He couldn't see more than a foot in front of his face through the downpour. A crashing came from the tree line, reminding him of deer hunting with his dad.

What spooked you? he wondered

He approached the driver door. "Damn it!" he yelled as his foot sunk deep into the mud, causing him to drop the flashlight. He couldn't see it, but he could hear it rolling down into the ditch. "Shit."

His leg had sunk nearly to the knee in the mud, and he was trying his hardest to work his leg free, cursing and mumbling.

More tree limbs snapped in the distance.

He couldn't see anything in the darkness aside from a yellow flashing on the ground from the rear of the vehicle.

"Wh-who's there?" he called.

All he heard was the sound of the rain.

He stared into the darkness, trying to let his eyes adjust. Placing his hands on the ground for support, he pulled on his left leg again, harder this time. The hole seemed to be eating his foot. Bones cracked and popped in his ankle as he repeatedly yanked on it. Finally, with much effort, his foot was extracted from the hole, but the mud had sucked off his shoe and he could already feel the cold water soaking his sock. He stumbled forward from the force of his leg being released, slamming his face into the driver door of the wrecked car. As blood ran in rivulets from his nose, he screamed in pain. His vision was shaky, and he tried to stand, using the car for support.

When he finally clambered to his feet again, he looked like he had just emerged from the Black Lagoon. Mud caked his uniform, blood ran from his face, and he was missing a shoe. Attempting to regain his composure, he looked into the driver's window. No one was in the vehicle—at least not that he could see. He cursed himself for dropping the flashlight and opened the door.

Carefully, he patted the driver's seat and made sure nothing—and no one—was in it. He sat in the car and felt for the dome light. He fumbled in the darkness, but finally, his fingers found the switch and he turned on the light, almost screaming when he saw all the blood.

He was sitting in it. The steering wheel was covered in it. It even coated the beer cans littering the floorboard.

"Jesus Christ," he gasped. "What the hell happened here?"

He decided to search the area more thoroughly, wondering if he was going to need to call an ambulance after all. None of the windows were broken, the windshield was intact, nobody had been ejected from the vehicle. Feeling stupid, he stepped out into the mud again with his shoeless foot first. He was starting to get the feeling that he shouldn't have touched anything at the scene.

"Hello?" he called. "Hello? I'm Deputy Dumear. I'm here to help."

Suddenly, a high-pitched whine like a distressed animal made him slowly turn and look over his shoulder to see a creature—*no, a man*—kneeling in front of him on all fours. The man wore multiple pelts crudely stitched together and draped over his slumped frame. A leather mask covered his face with fur stitched on it in ragged snatches. His eyes peered through the crude eyeholes. And, on top of his head, were horns.

"Listen," he said, holding his hands up. "Listen, now, I don't want any part of this. Okay, I mean, listen. You can go on now. I didn't see anything, okay?" He swallowed hard; his last cigarette tasted terrible in his mouth.

The Goatman blinked slowly. He lowered his head and bleated.

He felt warm urine trickle down his leg. His hand reached for his gun slowly. The Goatman's head and eyes followed his hand.

"Alright now, you be good now. Okay, I'm just—" the Goatman lowered his head and rammed Benny, slamming him into the car door. He fought to hold the horns away from his belly with one hand while his other hand—the hand that was reaching for the gun—was pinned against the side of the car by a hooved hand. He tried again to push the monster off him, but the beast was just too strong for him.

Slowly, the Goatman lowered his head further, as if bowing for prayer. Benny still struggled. "Please," he begged. "Please, I have three kids. And a..." The Goatman brought his head back up with such force that the deputy's abdomen was torn wide open, his insides foaming from his gaping belly. He squealed like a pig as blood poured from his mouth and nose. Dropping his limp corpse to the ground, the Goatman returned to the woods.

CHAPTER TWENTY-FIVE

Rain water trickled down into the cellar, causing the dirt on the floor to quickly turn to mud. Patrick, Sam, and John sat slumped against the wall farthest from the cellar door.

Patrick felt weak and dehydrated. He stood up slowly, in case the others were asleep, and walked over to the spot under the door. A steady stream of rainwater poured in there, and he was done asking himself if it was worth it. He positioned himself under the stream of water and drank. The water was cool and refreshing. He wondered if he would ever see the outside of this cellar again.

"Hey," John whispered. "Is it good?"

"Yeah," he answered. "It's better than nothing."

"I'm not feeling so good. What d'you think that was that we ate? Christ, I might have to shit in the corner."

His stomach flopped at the thought of sitting in this dank cellar with the smell of someone else's shit in his nose.

"I really don't know what it was," he said. "To be completely honest I'd rather not know. I would like to know what they're going to do with us, though."

"They're going to kill us," Sam said.

He was startled. He honestly had thought Sam had been asleep.

"No," he said, running his hands under the stream of water. "I don't plan on letting anyone hurt us at all."

"It will happen," Sam said. His voice was very monotone. Very matter-of-fact. "If it's not these people out here, it will be... him."

The three of them jumped when a shout came from the other side of the far wall.

"What was that?" John said. "I thought we were underground."

The shouting continued.

Patrick walked to the far wall and began feeling his hands along the boards. He wasn't sure what he was checking for exactly, but he had seen people do this in movies. John and Sam walked over to the wall and began tapping on it in different places.

"Here," John said. "It's hollow."

Patrick went to where John stood and rapped his knuckles against the wall.

Thonk.

"Let me out of here!" The voice screamed from the other side of the wall. "Let me go you fucking monsters! You can't do this to people!"

"Oh my God," John exclaimed.

"That's Tim," said Patrick.

———◆———

Sheriff Stanton had to drive at a snail's pace just to keep his car on the road. Elmer sat in the passenger's seat convulsing.

He swerved and said, "What in the hell is wrong with you, boy?"

Blood poured from the boy's nose splattering on the front of his pants. His eyes rolled up into the back of his head. Stanton pulled to the side of the road in a rush. "Are you okay, boy?" he asked.

Elmer stopped moving for a moment. Stanton could barely hear his breath leaving his lungs, but his chest wasn't moving.

"I'm sorry," he said suddenly. "Your deputy is dead."

"Benny? What do you mean he's dead?"

The rain pounded the roof of the car so hard that Stanton had to shout to be heard now.

Elmer sat forward and wiped his nose on his shoulder. "He's been killed. Just up here... over the hill."

Stanton eyed the boy, unsure what to say. The *swish-swish* of the windshield wipers was driving him crazy. "I'm going to go over the hill there," he said slowly. "And there ain't gonna be any problems."

Elmer didn't respond.

Stanton pulled the car over the hill and cursed under his breath. Turning on his lights, he parked behind Benny's car.

"Stay here," he said. Elmer was silent, holding a McDonald's napkin under his nose to staunch the blood. Opening his door, Stanton got out of the car and Elmer saw him every other second each time the rain was wiped away from the windshield. It was like a frame-by-frame picture show.

Flash: Stanton reaches Benny's driver door and looks in. *Flash:* his gun is drawn. *Flash:* Stanton's hands cover his mouth. *Flash:* Stanton runs back to the car.

"How the fuck could you know that?" he screamed as he opened his door. His was face contorted in sickened horror.

"I don't know," Elmer admitted. "But do you believe me now?"

<hr>

"What do we do?" John asked in the dark cellar.

Patrick paced along the wall that connected to the rest of the house. "I'm thinking," he said.

"Why can we hear Tim so well?" Sam said.

"What do you mean?"

"I mean, I know he was screaming, but it sounded like he was in here with us."

Patrick looked around the room, scanning every corner. "John, do you still have that lighter?"

"Yeah," John said as he dug in his pocket and handed him the lighter. Flicking it on, Patrick held it up high over his head. "There," he said, pointing above the paneling. "There's a vent."

"That's it!" John exclaimed. "We're going to get out of here!"

"I don't know. That hole is pretty small." He thought of Sam. He thought of how much weight he had lost this year. He didn't want to ask—

"I can fit through there," Sam said.

"I don't like it. It's not safe."

"Staying in here isn't safe. Staying in here means we die. You know it."

He did know it. He frowned, thinking of Dean. Why had he been so stubborn?

"You take this with you for light," he said, holding out the lighter. "Be careful, and don't let them see you. Just find a way to come let us out."

"Got it."

He was blown away by his little brother's courage. What would those dipshits who had picked on him all year say if they knew what he was really like?

"We'll have to boost him up," John said.

They both put their hands under Sam's feet and slowly pushed him up until his fingers gripped the edge of the vent.

"Just a little bit more," he said.

They stood on their toes now, using all their strength to balance him. With one final push, he successfully climbed into the hole. Once inside, he turned around and gave them a thumbs-up.

"Remember," Patrick said, "be as quiet as you can. Get outside and open the latch."

Sam nodded, turned, and he was gone.

Stanton didn't need any more convincing about Elmer's gift. Going against his better judgement and fully aware that his job would be on the line, he left the scene of the crime with Elmer.

"I can't believe I'm doing this," he said. "If anyone finds out I left the scene without calling it in... well, I don't have to tell you what would happen. But if I stay, there's no telling when I could leave. Probably be tied up for hours. And Benny..."

"I'm sorry about your friend. I didn't see that coming soon enough." Elmer stared at the floorboard.

"I don't blame you, son. But Benny was a good kid. He deserved better than that."

Turning left in the direction of the Coheelee Creek Covered Bridge, he continued. "Can we really stop it? These other kids. Can we stop them from dying?"

Elmer looked at Stanton, pretending not to notice the tears in his eyes and said, "I hope so."

CHAPTER TWENTY-SIX

S am only flicked the lighter on once. The vent was completely dark, and he needed to see where to go. First it curved right, then left, until it came to a stop. He crawled on his belly like a soldier storming the Normandy Beaches. His breath was shallow, and he fought to keep it as quiet as possible. Looking down through the open vent, Sam couldn't see much of anything. The room was in total darkness, and his eyes could just barely make out a table sitting below the vent.

If I'm lucky, he thought, *I can slide down onto the table without making too much noise.*

He wasn't sure what he was hearing, but it sounded like there were a dozen babies simultaneously sucking their bottles sounds in the room below. A smell emanated from the area that reminded him of the pig pen on his uncle's farm. He carefully positioned himself so that his stomach was facing down and his feet were facing out. Inch by inch, he worked his legs out of the vent until he felt the steel table under his toes. Working to gain his footing, he felt his foot knock against something and heard breaking glass. He heard startled moaning sounds and froze.

I don't have the upper body strength to pull myself back up, he thought as he let go of the ledge and quickly jumped down from the table.

He landed on his feet in what felt like mud. Flies swarmed around his face like paparazzi. The stench was almost unbearable now, and Sam tried not to gag. Finding the wall, he traced his way to the door.

He reached for the handle and almost turned it when he heard footsteps in the hall accompanied by the jingle of keys. There was a *click-click-click* as the key was inserted into the lock.

His breath choked in his throat. Still unable to see his surroundings, he did the only thing he could and hid behind the door.

———◦———

Sheriff Stanton parked his car in the same spot Gary Hall's Suburban had sat. The rain had finally stopped, but the ground was soaked, and the mud was deep.

"I'm going to leave the car running," he said to Elmer. "I'll keep the doors locked too, so you don't have to worry about anything."

"I'm not staying here. Absolutely not."

"Son, I can't be liable for what happens to you. I shouldn't have even let you get in the car in the first place."

"You need my help. Or, actually, I need your help. Remember that I came to you for help, I could have done this on my own. If you leave, I'll just follow behind you. I'm coming."

Stanton sighed. He pointed to the glovebox. "Well then, will you grab me a cigar? I need it like I need open heart surgery from a toddler but give it here anyway."

Elmer grabbed a cigar from the glovebox and handed it to him, then Stanton locked the car and turned on his flashlight. "Let's go," he said.

He shined his flashlight on the campground, but all he saw was an abandoned fire pit with some trash in it. "There's a trail up here," he said. "Does that seem right?"

"Yes," Elmer replied. "It feels right."

Brushing limbs out of his way, Stanton asked, "So what's your story, huh? How do you know the things you know?"

"I told you, I don't know. All I know is that it happens sometimes. Not very often, either."

"Is it always this serious? It's never just finding some poor family's lost dog?"

Elmer thought for a moment. "The first thing I remember happening was when I was six years old. My little brother and I shared bunk-beds. I woke up during the night and I saw my brother being crushed to death by the top bunk. I say *saw*, but I mean that it was more of a vision. Me being the older one, I had the top bunk, of course. I started smelling pennies and I noticed that I had a trail of blood coming out of my nose. I climbed down the ladder and checked on my brother, James. He was fine. I was so shaken up by the vision of his dead body that I had to wake him up. My parents said that it was just a bad dream and for us to both go back to bed. I just couldn't shake the image of James' sunken-in skull. I made him sleep on the couch with me. That night, the top bunk did fall onto the lower one. It broke in such a way that jagged pieces of wood and metal went straight through James' mattress, right where his pillow usually was."

Stanton whistled. "You're a hero, then. Really."

"It doesn't feel like it. It feels like I'm responsible for everything I can't stop. That's why I'm here. I couldn't stop it all, but I had to try."

There was a rustling in the woods, crackling leaves and snapping twigs. Drawing his gun, Stanton held his flashlight up above his shoulder.

"Hello?" he called.

A screeching sound came from behind them. Wheeling around, he shined the flashlight in the direction the noise had come from.

"Who's out here?"

After several moments, they continued on.

"I hate it out here," Stanton said. "I try to avoid it at all costs."

"Because there is something truly bad out here?"

"I don't know. Maybe. I've spent my entire time in the county telling myself that kids were just having fun, but I'm not so sure of that anymore."

They came to the clearing where the boys had been only hours earlier.

"Jesus," he continued. "Someone tried to burn this tree down."

The tree was blackened, many of the branches had fallen off and the entire bottom half of the tree was charred. "It looks like the rain stopped it before it could burn all the way up, though,"

"Could it be lightning that hit it?" Elmer said.

"I don't think so. It's just the bottom that's burned." Stanton walked under where the large branch had once stretched. Taking a few steps back, he looked up at its stump, then he got down on his knees and sifted through the ash and charred wood. After some time, he stood back up, clutching something in his hands.

"Goddamn this thing."

He held up a rope with a noose tied on the end. It was perfectly intact.

CHAPTER TWENTY-SEVEN

Sam held his breath as two men entered the room, Jeb and the one they called "Grandpa." The door swung open hard, stopping an inch in front of Sam's nose. Sam pressed his back tight against the wall, suddenly afraid that the two men might hear his heart beating.

The younger man jeered, "It's that time again, ladies!" He made sucking sounds with his mouth.

Pa smacked him in the back of the head. "Will you shut the fuck up?!" he whisper-shouted. "You know we don't talk during collection. What's gotten into you today? Do you know how much scrubbing Ma is having to do in the dining room because of you? And now you talk in front of the livestock."

"Sorry, Pa. They're dumb as rocks, though. I didn't think it'd hurt nothin'."

Pa reached the far side of the room and pulled a bronze chain, lighting the room a musty yellow. Sam shrank down to the floor. He could see under the stall closest to him. There was a woman on all fours, completely naked; her breasts were hanging down in miserable flaps. Connected to her nipples were clamps which were pumping up and down.

Oh my God, Sam thought. *This can't be real.*

Jeb started whistling, and Sam heard the clank of glass jars. The squishing of feet on the floor became louder, and he realized that he had to get out of there, fast.

Lowering himself to the floor, he could see everything. The girl had been forced onto all fours with some kind of metal contraption attached to her. Tubes ran from the pumps on her breasts and dripped into a metal bucket. A pair of boots entered the stall, and the girl began to make distressed noises. She sounded like a deaf person trying to speak.

"Shhhh," the man said.

Sam began to crawl to the doorway, praying that he wouldn't be seen. He made it around the door and began to back out of the room when the girl looked over at him. Her eyes wide, she began to scream.

"Shut her up!" Pa said from across the room.

Sam exited the room completely and stood up. His breath was sharp and his lungs hurt. He heard a loud thwack, and the screaming stopped.

He slunk down the dark hallway until he found the door which led into the dining room. It was locked. Sam turned around and went back the other way. Not wanting to pass the room he had just exited, he tested the only other door he could. Thankfully, it was unlocked. He opened the door, entered and shut it carefully behind him.

The room was lit with a small lamp in the far corner. In front of him, as if on display in the middle of the room, Tim lay on a metal table, naked except for his boxers. Leather straps were wrapped around his torso and legs.

"Tim," Sam whispered.

His friend turned his head slowly in his direction. He was very pale, and he seemed to be in a daze. Sam saw blood pooled under Tim's body on the table, a lot of it. He walked closer and saw why there was so much.

Both of his arms were missing. Crude bandages covered the stumps where his arms had once been. "Oh my God," Sam said. He didn't know what else to say.

Tim didn't respond.

He heard Pa say something to Jeb through the wall. Footsteps sounded as one of them entered the hallway.

Tim's eyes widened. His mouth opened and his tongue struggled to move. "Hide," he said in a faint voice.

Sam swung around wildly, looking for a place to hide. The footsteps were right outside the door. The knob turned and he dropped to the floor, rolling under a makeshift gurney against the wall. A bloody butcher's apron hung down in front of him like sheets hanging off a bed.

Jeb entered the room. "There you are!" he said. "Thanks for sticking around."

Tim stared at the ceiling.

"Hey boy," Jeb said. "I'm talking to you. Hey, did you know that some consider it a mortal sin to play with your pecker? Look, between you and me, I don't give a shit what you do. But in the middle of the woods? In our woods? There's kids running around. Our own Luna had to see that disgrace of a prick you've got with her own eyes."

Tim had lost so much blood that he couldn't even tell if he still had his "prick." He wanted to die.

"So now, you don't have to worry about it anymore, unless you're one of those freaks who can suck his own cock. You are, aren't you? Hey, who hasn't tried it, right?"

Pa walked into the room. "Jeb, quit fuckin' around and help me. He's brought us a dead one. Finish up here so we can get to cutting."

"Yes, sir," Jeb said.

Pa turned and left the room. Jeb turned back to Tim. "Discount on aisle five!" He said with a laugh. "Hey, frozen is cheaper for a reason. But, as the song says, you can't always get what you want."

Jeb started to untie the leather straps that held Tim down. "Do you remember the knife?" He said. "The one I used on your arms?"

Tim looked dead already. He didn't answer.

"I know you can hear me, so I'll just say it. If you struggle, it'll be your balls I cut off next."

Jeb opened a deep freezer behind him and moved things to the side. He turned, undid the straps around Tim's ankles, and picked his body up like he was carrying Christ to his tomb. Only, Tim wouldn't be rising in three days.

Jeb held Tim's body over the freezer. He leaned close to Tim's ear. "The soup was delicious," he said. "Your friends enjoyed it, too." He dropped Tim's body into the freezer and shut the lid. He pulled a key from his pocket, shoved it into the freezer's locking mechanism, and turned.

Sam held his hands over his mouth. Tears ran down his face. Jeb left the room and Sam had to listen to the banging from the inside of the freezer until it stopped. It was the longest few minutes of Sam's life.

Stanton and Elmer stood in the clearing, staring up at the burned tree. Looking at Elmer, Stanton asked "Which way do we go from here?"

"I'm not a bloodhound."

"How am I supposed to know how it works?"

Elmer's eyes grew large and he pointed behind the sheriff. A small girl in a dress was staring at them.

"Hey!" Stanton called.

The girl turned and darted into the woods.

"Hey, stop!" He shined his flashlight in her direction. "Come on!" he said as they followed her into the woods.

Sam hated himself. He wished he wasn't such a pussy. Maybe he could have stopped Jeb from tossing Tim into the freezer. But no, he had just cowered and waited for his friend to die. Deep down though, he knew there was nothing he could have done. He just needed to get out of the house. He could hear grunting and shuffling of feet coming down the hall.

"Car crash," Pa said. "He got us another one. Said there was another one too, but he could only drag one at a time."

"He needs to be more careful," Jeb said. "Plus, we've got enough on our plate already." He laughed.

They entered the room, carrying a dead man. Jeb carried the arms, and Pa, the legs. They laid the body on the table. "You know the deal," Pa said. "He's just holding up his end."

"We haven't had a birth in months, though," Jeb said.

"Doesn't matter. He's forgiving. He knows we're working on it."

The left hand of the dead man hung off the side of the table. Sam could see a wedding ring.

"Here," Pa said, approaching the far side of the table. "Help me turn him."

Jeb walked around to where Pa stood and helped him roll the man onto his side. As they worked to pull the man's shirt off, Sam could see the man's face. He had only met him once, but he knew instantly that it was Ronnie Garland.

CHAPTER TWENTY-EIGHT

Pa raised the hacksaw as Jeb held Ronnie's arm steady. Sam covered his eyes and tried to imagine that he was somewhere else, even back at school locked in a locker for the entire day. He didn't care, as long as it was anywhere but here in this room with these murderous psychopaths.

There was a knock from the front door. And again. And again. Louder each time. "Let me in!" came Luna's voice.

"Damn," Pa said. "Is she going for a new record tonight?"

"I'll go let her in," Jeb said, sighing.

He walked out of the room, and Sam heard his keys jingle as he unlocked the hallway door. Moments later, he heard the front door open. Pa had begun to saw off Ronnie's arm. Sick, crunching sounds nearly caused Sam to cry out in horror.

"Pa!" called Jeb.

He kept working as if he hadn't heard him.

"Pa! Come here, damn you!"

"I'm working! What is it?" Pa shouted back. He mumbled something under his breath which Sam was pretty sure was the word "worthless."

"Pa!" Jeb shouted again. "Luna saw a cop. He's headed this way."

Pa dropped the hacksaw on the table and let go of Ronnie's limp arm. "Goddamnit!" he yelled and stormed out of the room.

"You wait right here," Stanton said to Elmer. They were hidden in the trees a hundred yards away from the house. "I mean it."

"Can't you call for help or backup or something?" Elmer asked.

"My backup is slumped on the ground on Highway 52 with his guts on the outside of his body. Besides, what would I tell them? That a creepy little girl ran away from me? That I found some rope in an ash pit? Just stick close, kid."

"Right," Elmer said, feeling stupid. "Okay, but if I hear a gunshot or something, I—"

"You'll what? No offense, kid, but there isn't much you can do. Just let me do my job, I'll get to the bottom of it."

"Okay, but what about the Goatman? He could be out here."

"He could be in there," Stanton said, before walking away from their hiding spot and approaching the door. His hand on his gun, he knocked loudly.

He could hear people talking inside. He stepped back a couple paces from the doorway when he heard someone unlocking the deadbolt. The door opened, and a little girl stood in the doorway.

"Hi there," he said. "I'm Sheriff Paul Stanton. Are you the little girl I saw back that way, in the clearing?"

Luna nodded. He tried looking past her, but the house was too dark to see much of anything.

"Well, you didn't have to run, you know. I'm a good guy, okay?"

Luna just looked at him.

Stanton was getting frustrated.

"Listen," he said. "I need to ask you something, okay? I need to know if everything is okay here. Can you tell me that? You can nod for yes, or shake your head for no. Okay?"

The little girl's eyes seemed to peer right through his own. For just an instant, it seemed like she was going to nod her head when an old man came to the door.

"Well, hey there, Sheriff," Pa said. "Sure is late! What can I do ya for?"

"Sir," Stanton said. "Do you mind if I come in? I'd just need a minute of your time."

Pa's eyes flicked to Stanton's gun. He still had his hand on the holster's release mechanism. "Heh, sorry," He said, releasing his gun. "It's been a rough night."

"I completely understand. My granddaughter has taken to wandering off in the night. You can imagine my worry. Almost drives an old man to drinking. Come on in, Sheriff. We can get you something to eat. Are you hungry?"

Stepping through the doorway, Stanton said, "No thank you. I've just got some questions, that's all."

"Fair enough."

The old man led him into the dining room. "Have a seat," he said.

Stanton glanced around the room. The stench of the place forced its way into his very soul. There were towels draped onto the table and floor.

"I'll stand, thank you."

Pa's eyes narrowed the slightest bit.

"Is it just you two here?" Stanton asked. "You and the girl?"

"My wife is sleeping in the bedroom. She isn't well, and she sleeps more than I knew a person could," he said with a chuckle.

"So, there's just the three of you, then?"

"That's right."

"Listen, I'll cut right to the chase here. I'm looking for some kids. Teenagers. Have you seen any around here?"

"Hell, we never see anyone out here. Nope. Sorry, Sheriff. I won't be able to help you there."

"I see," Stanton said.

———————

Sam crawled slowly out from under the gurney. He stood up and checked the door. It was unlocked. Holding his breath, he slowly turned the handle. He could hear the Sheriff talking in the other room. All he would have to do is shout, and this would all be over. Or would it? He had heard the Sheriff asking questions and Pa was answering them. But where was Jeb?

He slipped into the hallway and stood face to face with Luna. Her eyes widened, but she knew better than to scream.

"Shhhh," he said, holding a finger to his mouth. "Please."

For a moment, the two stared at each other in silence. Luna looked towards the door that led to the kitchen. She looked back at Sam.

"Please," he whispered again. "Just pretend you didn't see me."

Luna turned, walked down the hall, and back into her bedroom.

He felt a wave of relief wash over him. He stood in the dark hallway a moment longer, before returning to the room where Ronnie's body lay. Walking around to the back side of the room, he saw a screwdriver on a table and put it in his back pocket.

———————

"Well, Sheriff," Pa said. "I hate that we couldn't be more of a help to you, but it's getting late. I need to be checkin' on Ma now."

"I understand," Stanton said. "But surely you wouldn't mind if I checked around the house real quick? Just to ease my mind."

Pa's face contorted into an awful grimace. Nobody had ever been in this house and left to tell about it. The Sheriff would be no different.

"Something wrong?"

"Of course not. You lead the way. Door to the hallway is right there." He pointed behind Stanton.

Stanton gave him a faint smile and reached for the door handle. As he turned the handle and opened the door, Pa shuffled behind him into the hallway.

He peered into the dark hallway, squinting. "Could you guys be so kind as to turn on a light?" he said. There was no answer. He turned around and was struck in the face with a shovel. Falling backwards, his head slammed into the floor. He turned to the left in an attempt to roll away and saw a young boy standing just around the corner. With one hand, Sam held a finger to his lips while the other hand clutched a screwdriver. Before Stanton could move, the shovel came down hard on his ankle and he heard his bones break. He screamed in pain then blacked out.

Pa stood over his body and held the shovel above his throat. "I'm going to carve out your Adam's apple now, you nosy bastard," Pa said.

Sam lunged out of the corner at a full run and slammed Pa into the wall, knocking the shovel to the floor. Screaming and clawing, Pa kicked at Sam. His long fingernails left a scratch across the boy's cheek. Sam kneed him in the stomach, knocking him back, and drove the screwdriver into the old man's chest with as much force as he could muster. Pa lunged at him and the screwdriver plunged further into his torso, the dull tip somehow finding its way all the way into the old man's heart.

Sam felt it beating through the handle.

The old man knew it too, the way he looked down at it, the blood spilling out of his mouth, his heart weakening and still beating against the screwdrivers' dull point.

Sam let go of it and stumbled back, gasping for breath as he saw Pa weakly twist at the handle and try to pull it out. When it was clear that it was of no use, the old man staggered towards him, coughing blood.

Sam stepped forward and grabbed the handle again. He yanked it free and drove the screwdriver into the old man's jugular.

Pa hit the floor.

———◦———

Elmer couldn't wait any longer. Out in the woods, he felt like an open target. There were noises all around him. Unsure of what he could even do, he left his hiding spot and approached the front door. His heart felt like it was going to burst in his chest when the floorboards of the steps groaned.

"Oh shit," he whispered to himself. He tried peeking inside, but the windows were all tightly boarded up. Reaching for the tarnished brass doorknob, he stopped with the distinct feeling that he was being watched. He waited only a moment before he rattled it.

Locked.

Someone screamed inside the house. He looked for cracks in the boarded-up windows but couldn't find anything. "Shit, shit," he muttered under his breath. Jumping from the porch, he made his way around the side of the house where he found a storm cellar with a thick metal lock holding the doors shut.

Elmer approached the doors and called, "Hello?"

"Sam?" a voice replied. "Oh, thank God!"

"No. I'm not Sam. I'm—" his voice trailed off.

"What's going on?" A different voice called. "Hello?"

Elmer didn't respond. To his left, something else had caught his attention. Hair stood on the back of his neck as he made out the figure of the Goatman peering at him from between two trees. Covered in blood and gore, the creature stared intently at him with two almost-human eyes. The body of Deputy Benny Dumear lay on the ground next to him. A trail of blood streaked behind them through the leaves.

The Goatman's beady eyes stayed focused under his leather-knit mask. His chin was covered with thick, bristly hair. He bleated loudly and his jaw snapped closed as he took a prowling step forward, snorting loudly into the air.

Oh, you gotta be fucking kidding me...

More calls from the cellar. Elmer was frozen in place. He could see an axe leaning against a tree stump about halfway between himself and the monster. Neither of them moved.

I can outrun him. I have to.

He could see the horns. He could see the eyes. A chill went down his spine. The malformed brute made another bleating sound and shook his head from side to side. Ready to explode with adrenaline, he took off towards the axe. The monster ran too, at an incredible speed, his head lowered and ready to charge. Reaching the stump just before it, he grabbed the axe and swung it up with both arms. The Goatman didn't slow his charge as Elmer held the axe in front of him in defense. The curled horns slammed into the wood of the axe, splintering the handle and throwing him backwards.

He hit the ground. *Hard.*

Scrambling to stand back up, he realized that he had dropped the axe and it was now out of his reach. The

Goatman backed up, let out a rough, snorting breath, and charged again like an angry bull.

Elmer wasn't ready to die like this.

Acting on instinct and gathering all his will in desperation, he drew upon the power he had always suspected was inside him. Holding his hands in front of him, he commanded the hellish beast to stop. There was no time to think of what would happen, but he tried anyway.

The Goatman froze in his tracks as if he had run into an invisible wall. He let out an inhuman roar of frustration and clawed at the air in front of him. Blood streaked from Elmer's nose, and the veins at his temples thumped violently. He held one hand in the monster's direction while he picked up the axe with his other. He walked to where the cellar door was and slammed the blade into the lock three times. Patrick and John erupted from the cellar and froze in horror.

"It's him," John said. "Oh God."

Elmer was pale and shaky. Cold sweat dripped from his forehead.

Patrick stumbled over to him. "How the hell are you doing that?"

The Goatman was suspended in the air now, inches above the ground. Blood slowly dripped onto the dirt.

"Run," was the only word he could muster. The two boys gave each other a glance before taking off around the front of the house.

Elmer grew weak, and he knew he couldn't hold the beast back much longer. He gave a push with his hand and that was all he had left. The horned freak fell back a few feet, then charged at him again—this time faster and harder.

Barely able to stand, he waited until the Goatman was close enough and took his best swing with the axe. The blade sank into the back of its head with a wet splat.

Flailing and thrashing wildly, the monster pawed in agony at the axe embedded in its skull. The creature's primal screams echoed through the woods. He fell backwards to the ground, his neck jerking roughly as his head slammed into the hard earth.

His vision went dark.

He heard ragged breaths. The dragging of limbs. Someone was screaming.

Struggling to function, he stumbled to a crouching position and saw the Goatman standing over him, blood trickling down the front of his horrible mask, leaking from his eye sockets. There he stood for a while, his body waving forwards and backwards. Then, making a gruff sound of pain, he fell. Without giving himself time to think, Elmer ran to where the Goatman lay, and stomped as hard as he could on the head of the axe. The blade sank deep into the monstrous skull. A spray of blood and brain matter went flying, splattering his face and shirt.

The screaming in his ears, he realized, was his own voice.

CHAPTER TWENTY-NINE

"We have to go back and help him," John said.

"I have to find Sam first!" Patrick nearly screamed.

They reached the front of the house, and found the front door hanging open.

"You do what you want. I'm going to find my brother."

John stared at him for just a moment before turning and going back the way he came. Patrick entered the house and started screaming for Sam.

Heading back around the side of the house, John found Elmer lying on the ground next to the bloody body of the Goatman. "Elmer," he said, shaking him. "Come on man, get up." The other boy sat up slowly and John helped him to his feet.

"I don't know how or why you're here," John said. "But thank you."

"Don't mention it," he said. "Hold on." He walked over to the massive corpse and stuck his foot on the back of its neck. With both hands, he pulled the axe from its head with a sick sound like a spoon through a bowl of coleslaw. The Goatman didn't move.

"Let's go," Elmer said.

Inside the house, Sam was trying to wake Sheriff Stanton.

"Sam!" Patrick called again.

"In here!" Sam called back from the hallway.

Patrick opened the door leading into the hallway and saw the grotesque scene. The old man was slumped against the wall face-first with a screwdriver in his throat, the Sheriff's foot was demolished, and Sam looked shell-shocked.

"Come on, Sam," he said. "Come on, we're leaving right now."

"We can't leave yet," Sam said. "There are people here who need help."

"I don't care, Sam," he said, "we've got to—"

Patrick's eyes flew out of his head as a pitchfork penetrated the back of his skull. His mouth tried to move, but no sounds came out. Sam screamed as the pitchfork was jerked violently, and the top half of his brother's head was separated from the bottom half with a sickening crunch. He panicked. All the hero in him was completely spent. Taking off running, he banged on Luna's door.

"Please," he cried. "Please don't let him do this."

"Come on," Jeb said. "Eye for an eye, what do you say? In this case, I guess you could say eyes, right? Goddamn, boy. That wasn't your brother, was it?"

Jeb laughed and kept coming down the hallway. Sam was certain he was about to die a pretty gruesome death.

Then he heard the gunshot.

From the front page of the *Early County Daily*:

AN EXERCISE IN TERROR

Early County has been rocked to its core in a recent grisly discovery. Eight reported dead so far, and countless more bodies have been discovered packed into freezers and various other locations. The lead officer who worked the crime scene described it as the "worst possible scenario you could ask for in this line of work." The officer, who wishes to remain nameless, said that the eight dead were the least disturbing thing about the case. Among the victims discovered was the body of Deputy Ben Dumear.

Story continues on page 2A.

CHAPTER THIRTY

W*hat else is there to say? When it comes down to it, I don't know what talking about it will do. Kay says she thinks I ought to do the talk show, though. She says it would be good for me to get it all out there. I guess I will do it. I just don't feel good about it is all.*

They want to know all the details. They want to squeeze every last drop of information out of me. I've avoided interviews this long. God knows I wish I could avoid them until the end of time, but money talks. The bills are piled up, I've got three kids' college tuitions to pay for, and I figure, Hell, some words on TV, and our problems get a lot less problematic. I practically have to do it.

Jeb's body fell to the floor in a lifeless heap. Sam slumped into the corner in the dark hallway and held his face in his hands. Stanton held his gun at the ready, waiting for another backwoods piece of shit to try him. He made the mistake of looking down at his ankle and saw that his foot was barely attached anymore. He tried not to think about it.

"Hey," he said to Sam. "Are you okay?"

"No."

"I mean, are you hurt?"

"No." But Sam would never be the same.

Elmer and John walked through the front door and saw Patrick's body slumped against the hallway doorframe.

"Holy shit," John said. He turned his head and vomited violently.

Stanton called out, "Hey kid, is that you?"

"Yeah," Elmer said. "It's me. He's dead, Sheriff. The Goatman. He's dead."

Stanton turned to Sam, "Who else is here?" he asked.

"There's the little girl in here," Sam said pointing to the door next to him. And there's the old lady, 'Ma'. That's all who's alive anymore, I think."

"You boys need to get out of here. That crazy bitch could be standing in the next room with a shotgun."

"I'm not leaving you," Elmer said. "We're not leaving you," he added, glancing toward John and Sam.

"He's right," John said. "We need to find her. We need to make sure."

Stanton considered it for only a moment. "Here," he said, handing Elmer his pistol. "Be careful."

"Stay here with him," John said to Sam. "We'll check out the rest of the house."

John picked up a knife and followed Elmer down the hall. The room at the end, the one Sam had seen Luna exit and enter, was locked. Turning, they crossed the dining room, only to be startled when they heard the scratch of a needle on a record player. An old tune from the 1950s bellowed from the open door beyond the dinner table.

Elmer's hand shook as he reached for the slightly-open door. He pushed the knob and it slowly swung open.

In the bed sat Ma in a relaxed position. She was wearing what appeared to be an ancient wedding gown, stained in blood.

The needle scratched on the warped record, as the old singer's words became slower and slower.

I'm wild again.
Beguiled again.
A simpering, whimpering child again.
Bewitched, bothered and bewildered am I.

The woman looked over at the two boys in the doorway and raised a rusty pistol from beneath the folds of her bloody dress.

"I was hoping to have peace for this," she said. "And don't try to understand what happened here. No one will ever know the truth."

And then she put the barrel of the gun in her mouth and pulled the trigger.

———◦———

Stanton called everyone he knew to call. He needed an ambulance immediately. Sam still hadn't told anyone what he had seen in the room with the girls. He couldn't bring himself to talk about it. Elmer and John waited in the house with them until more police showed up.

When the red and blue lights came through the front door, the group sighed a collective sigh of relief. Stanton filled the officers in on everything he knew, and the premises were searched thoroughly

Luna's bedroom window was open, the girl gone.

Stanton was lifted onto a stretcher. As they carted him into the ambulance, a young deputy approached him. His name tag identified him as Wilson.

"Sheriff," Deputy Wilson said. "Sheriff, I have to ask you something."

The EMT stepped aside, annoyed.

He continued, "Didn't you say that goat guy was supposed to be around here somewhere?"

"Yeah, he had an axe planted in his head."

"That's what I thought you said, sir. Um... Sir, he's nowhere on the property."

Stanton's eyes widened. He didn't speak. The young deputy said, "I just wanted to make sure I heard you right, sir." And he walked away.

———————◦◦———————

Stanton lay in a hospital bed in Dothan, Alabama with his leg wrapped and elevated. The TV was playing an old slasher movie. His face was sore from the broken nose he had suffered when hit in the face by the shovel, but nothing in his life had ever hurt as much as his foot did right then.

He was still in a daze, though. He could remember being wheeled back into the operating room, and the nurse telling him to count backwards from ten. He remembered the old doctor coming into his room and telling him he would never walk on his foot again. The doctor had informed him that it had been all but completely severed by the shovel, and you could say that he had taken the news well in the sense that he hadn't said anything at all. He figured the doctor must have been relieved that he hadn't broken down like most people did when they received terrible news. He figured he'd give the guy a break. Besides, he had always been the "suffer in silence" type.

A young male nurse entered the room. "Well, hey there!" he said. "Nice to see you alert this morning".

Glancing at the TV, he made a sour face. Jason was ripping some poor teenager open with a machete. The nurse picked up the remote and changed the channel.

Stanton thought of saying that it had just been getting good, but he didn't have the energy for humor anymore.

Another nurse entered the room. "Sheriff Stanton," she said. "There's quite the crowd out in the waiting room to see you. Are you feeling up to having visitors?"

"Sure," he said, though he couldn't imagine who would be waiting to see him. He had no family, no wife, and no real friends now that Benny was dead.

"Okay, I'll have them come in one at a time," the nurse said. "We don't want to overdo it."

Both nurses left the room and he was alone for a moment. Looking out the window, he could see that summer was in full swing. In the south, you can almost literally see how blisteringly hot it is outside during the summer.

On the TV, Charlotte the spider was trying to warn Wilbur the pig what the farmer actually does with pigs. "It's just how things are," she said.

A woman knocked on the door, and Stanton immediately knew two things about her: first was that she had a battered quality to her, a strong woman but another suffer in silence type. The second thing he noticed was that she was immensely beautiful. "Sheriff Stanton," she said. "I know you don't know me, but I owe a lot to you." In her hand was a bouquet of flowers tied together with a ribbon. She was wearing a black dress.

"Is that right?" he said, sitting up a little straighter. He winced when his leg moved.

She glanced at his bandaged leg. "Is it bad?" she said.
"It is."

"I'm so sorry to hear that," she said. "Well, let me tell you why I'm here. You saved my boy out in those terrible woods. John may never forget what he went through, but I will never forget what you did for him."

"Thank you for that. But it wasn't just me who had a hand in saving him. There was another boy who helped lead me to those kids."

"Yes. He's in the waiting room now. He can't wait to talk to you. He's been up here almost non-stop since you came out of surgery. He seems like a great young man. I'm curious though, how exactly did he know the boys would find trouble? John says that he tried to warn them."

"Ma'am, I wish I knew. But he was right about everything. He's a hero," he said, remembering the bunk beds.

"Well," the woman said. "I've got a funeral to get to now, but I just had to stop by here and tell you how much I appreciate you." She reached out to shake his hand.

"Funeral?"

"Yeah," she said. "My husband. His name was Ronnie."

He lowered his eyes. "I'm sorry to hear that."

"You know what's so crazy? It seems like such a cliché to say 'don't be,' but that's honestly all I can say. Ronnie was a very bad man, Mr. Stanton. That's all there is to it."

"I understand," he said. The woman turned to leave the room, and he called after her, "What's your name?"

The woman turned and smiled. "I'm Kay," she said. She set the flowers among the other flowers and cards and left the room.

―――――◦―――――

Kay and I were married two years later, and we still are to this day. She really is an amazing woman. She puts up with all my bullshit, and that's saying a lot. She is great at helping me get around, too. Yep, I'm still crippled. I'd be lost without her.

John went through a lot of counseling over the incident, and he turned out okay. He's a banker in Atlanta now. We named Kay and Ronnie's child after

Kay's father, Stan, and we had a child of our own three years after that. We named him Benny.

Sam Hall, that poor kid. He went through it all and came out a hell of a lot stronger for it. He's in his twenties now, has a wife and a kid of his own. Sam's father, Gary, drank himself to death about five years after Patrick died.

There is someone who's been on my mind for a long time now, and I can't find him. If there's one thing I learned in all my years in law enforcement, it's how to find someone. I worry about him a lot. We spoke on and off for years, but after some time, we just lost touch. I hope he's okay. He really was a fine young man.

———◦———

Within a few moments of Kay leaving Stanton's hospital room, there was another knock at the door.

"Come in," he said.

In walked Elmer with a sheepish grin on his face.

"What the hell are you smiling at?" Stanton said with a smile of his own.

Elmer glanced down at the chair by the door. He looked at Stanton. "You're in my room," he said.

"No, my chart is on the door. They let me see it. I get gold stars if I eat all of my applesauce."

Elmer laughed. He asked, "How are you feeling?"

"Terrible."

"Yeah, I figured you would tell me that."

"I'm only truthful with folks I trust. Consider yourself lucky."

"Hey, I'm sorry for what happened to you. I feel responsible for everything that happened."

"You're no more responsible for what happened than Elvis is responsible for 9/11. You helped save lives."

"We did," Elmer corrected him.

"Yeah, we did. And we also made sure nothing can happen to anyone else in that house ever again."

Elmer stared at the floor.

"Hey," Stanton continued. "I reckon I ought to stop callin' you 'boy,' and I sure as hell ain't callin' you Elmer, so, do you have a nickname?"

Elmer laughed. Leave it to Stanton to say what he really thought. "No," he said. "I've never had a nickname. And Elmer was my great-grandfather."

"Great Grandfather, terrible name." He thought for a moment and recalled Elmer's little brother, James, and how Elmer had saved him. "How about Bunk?" he said. "You look like a Bunk."

———◆———

Stanton was surprised at how excited he was to return to work. Even with the constant stream of visitors, three months out of work had been far too long. The absence of Benny was jarring, though. There was a framed picture of him on one wall of the room with an American flag hanging above it. He smiled and went over to the wall. He saluted the picture of his friend, feeling silly. But it just felt right to pay him respects. He was a military man after all.

There was a new Deputy starting that day, and he wanted to go check something before he arrived.

After pouring some coffee for the road, he limped to his car, still trying to get used to the crutches. He started the car and drove to the Coheelee Creek Campgrounds. The reports had said that the Goatman had never been found, and no one had seen the young girl, Luna, either, but he had one place he wanted to check that wasn't in the report.

Arriving several minutes later, he got out of his car, grabbed his crutches from the backseat, and began limping towards the woods.

EPILOGUE

The perky young host for *Good Morning America* sat forward and chewed on one of the arms of her glasses dramatically. "And what did you find in those woods?" she said. The audience waited with bated breath.

"You know what I found," Stanton said. "That's why I'm here, isn't it?"

Cheeks flushing, the girl said, "Oh come on now Sheriff, not everyone knows the full story of the Coheelee Cannibals. Tell the audience what you found."

He wished that he hadn't taken that third swig of whiskey backstage. He turned to the camera. "In the woods, I found the noose hanging from the tree again."

The audience gasped and he could see more than half the crowd were using their phones to record him. Hanging on to every word, thirsty for a good story.

"Hanging from the noose," he continued, "was the body of the girl named Luna. To this day, we don't have a last name for her."

"Because she was born right there in that house," the girl said, excitedly. "There was no record of her. Isn't that right?"

"That's right," he responded. Already, he was regretting his decision to come on the show.

He could see Kay, John, Benny, and Stanley standing offstage. Kay gave him a thumbs-up. He continued, "The girl was completely naked, except for a suit made of goat fur, horns, and hooves. The goat-suit was presumably the same one the Goatman wore. It was draped over her body."

Gasps.

The interviewer paused for effect. She continued, "Many people believe that the young girl was acting as this 'Goat Man' the whole time. What is your opinion on that, Mr. Stanton?"

"It's horseshit."

The interviewer flinched. She glanced at her producer who was making the signal for commercial break.

"When we return," she said, "We will continue this horrific story." The cameraman gave an 'OK' symbol.

"What are you doing?" the girl said to him. "You can't use language like that on live television."

"I'm sorry, sweetie. I was under the impression that you wanted to hear the uncensored story."

"Well, the gritty, gory details are fine, as we said before the show. Just keep the language out of it."

The cameraman put his headphones back on and gave the interviewer another signal.

"And we're back. Now, Mr. Stanton, please tell us about what was discovered in the house."

He paused for a moment and looked into the camera. If they wanted gritty and gory, they would get it. And they would never invite him back to be on *Good Morning America*—or any other show—that was for sure.

"The house was a farm for humans," he said. "There were a dozen females of ages ranging from thirty down to thirteen. Each of them completely feral, mentally retarded, and inbred. There were machines attached to them constantly which milked their breasts. The milk was sold to a local market for years. The men of the house, the ones they called 'Pa' and Jeb took turns raping the girls repeatedly, keeping them pregnant. The women who endured this torturous life have all since died... Many died while still being milked and raped."

The interviewer tried to interrupt. "Mr. Stanton—"

"When it came time for the babies to be born," he continued on, ignoring her, "if they were girls, they were raised strictly for the milking. Nobody ever talked in front of them to keep them as animalistic as possible."

"And what about the male children?" the reporter asked.

He sat back in his chair. "All killed," he said. "The official story is that they were buried behind the house, but some believe that they were sacrificed to an entity of some sort. But, ultimately, they were of no use to the 'farmers'... so they were killed. We found more than..." He took a deep breath. "We found more than thirty infant skeletons."

All eyes in the crowd were on their cellphone screens, capturing this piece of history.

"And the freezers?"

"There was another room. Like a butcher's cutting room. This is where the... meat was stored. We found body parts in bags and jars. We found packages labeled with names like 'ribs' and 'backstraps'."

A few people from the audience made shrieking sounds. One lady started walking toward the exit, holding her hand over her mouth.

"Is this why you decided to go vegan?" the girl said.

"I don't put a label on what I do," he answered.

"But is it?"

After a moment, he said, "Yes. I stopped eating animals after I saw what I saw. Wouldn't you?"

"I'm not sure I understand what you mean?" the girl said.

"I think I'm done."

The camera panned to the interviewer. "We'll be right back after these quick messages," she said.

She turned to him. "You have a contract with us. You are not done."

"To hell with the contract," he said. "I will not be questioned about my life choices on live television. I thought we agreed, no talk about the diet. That's not why I came on this show. I didn't come here to talk about myself."

"What would you like to talk about?" The camera was already rolling, she had missed the signal.

"Let's talk about humanity," he said. "Let's talk about the world we live in now."

"Okay. Though I'm not sure how this relates to the Coheelee Cannibals."

"I saw humans treated like livestock. I saw what humans are capable of that summer. I saw pure evil, and it wasn't from some demonic entity. And I was sitting in the hallway before this interview thinking, it isn't getting any better. People kill each other for no reason. People treat each other terribly every day, spewing hate every chance they get. Do you know that I watched you yell at a homeless man today on your way inside the building?"

"Excuse me?"

"And then, in your little segment before I came out here, you were begging the audience for donations for some huge organization. The CEO of that company is a millionaire and we're giving them millions of dollars while ignoring our fellow man in our hometowns."

"You can't say that," she said, looking towards her producer. The producer made the 'keep rolling' sign.

"He's not going to tell you to stop. It's all about ratings. Everything everyone does is for their own gain, that's my point. Even churches are guilty of this."

"Do you have a point?"

"Hell, I don't even know." Maybe he was regretting that drink a little too much. "You know what, you're right. Let's talk about my diet. You want those details, don't you? Ratings. Because that's all ratings are, right? Meat. That's what you are. Meat. That's what I am. Meat." He could feel the drink getting heavier in his stomach, his words slurring slightly, but he didn't care to stop. "That's what they are too. Meat." He pointed out to the crowd, even as they trained their cameras on him. "That's what they don't understand. Ultimately, if there is one thing I've learned in my lifetime, it's the inconvenient truth that we humans are nothing more than meat.

We're all just tamer animals."

THE END

August 2016-August 2017

FROM THE AUTHOR

I was seventeen years old. I had a friend who worked at the same skating rink/pizza place that I did. He was constantly berated and made fun of for being a vegetarian. He would always just smile, laugh it off, and go about his day. One day I asked him, "So, why *are* you a vegetarian? Why wouldn't you eat meat?" And he said he really didn't like to talk about it, so I dropped it. A couple months later, he said, "Do you still want to know why I'm a vegetarian?" And of course, I said yeah, because I thought he was crazy, missing out on so many foods. So, he says, "I was in the army. I was stationed in the middle-east, and you know that smell, when you drive by barbecue places?" I nodded, and he says, "Well, piles of burning human bodies smell exactly like that."

I don't tell you this to make you feel a certain way. You see, when I began writing *Tamer Animals,* I was indeed vegan. Initially, I felt like the story would go in a different direction, but I throttled it back a bit and it naturally fell into its own thing. In the genre of horror, you find that, much like the opening line of the novel, it's dangerous business stepping out your front door. After the craziness of *The Variant*, I wanted to write something more grounded in reality. Something with grit. I admit I was really digging *No Country for Old Men* by Cormac McCarthy and Sheriff Paul Stanton was heavily inspired by that story. But more than that, was the album and song of the same name by the band Other Lives. That line, *we're just tamer animals, we're the same as animals* really hit a nerve with me, and I mean in more ways than one, just like the double meaning in the book. I will say this about the big cannibalism reveal: it's there to support a story about real people dealing with real issues in their everyday life. You have homophobia, racism, violence, malice, and all-around hatred occurring in every city, every day, and it's not getting better. This book formed in my head as a metaphor for how violent we are towards animals. It ended as a realization that we're not any better to each other. I hope you enjoyed this book. If you did, do me a huge favor and rate it on Amazon and Goodreads. Also, if you enjoyed it, check out my other books, *The Variant* and *Candy*.

Until next time,
Justin

Want a FREE Story?

Haven't had enough Justin M. Woodward yet? How about a mailing list exclusive story? Head over to JustinMWoodward.com for your free story, *Mommy Drinks Because You're Bad.*

JUSTIN M. WOODWARD

MOMMY DRINKS BECAUSE YOU'RE BAD

A SHORT STORY

ABOUT THE AUTHOR

Justin M. Woodward is an author from Headland, Alabama. He lives with his wife and two small boys, Nathan and Lucas. Writing since 2015, *Tamer Animals* is his third full-length novel. You can keep up with him on social media, and on www.justinmwoodward.com

Follow him on his social media accounts:

Twitter: www.twitter.com/justinmwoodward

Instagram: www.instagram.com/justinmwoodward

Facebook: www.facebook.com/justinmwoodwardfiction

What to read next? Well, I highly recommend the prequel to the book you just read, *Rotten Little Things*.

"ROTTEN LITTLE THINGS takes you to some frightfully dark places." - Jay Sigler, author of TRAIN THOUGHTS

TWELVE YEARS BEFORE THE EVENTS OF TAMER ANIMALS

Monica has suffered from paranoid schizophrenia her entire life. For the most part, she manages her disease well—that is, until her family moves into an old house in the woods, and she starts seeing an imaginary entity from her childhood creeping around the property.

NEW HOME. OLD HAUNTS.

Things quickly become terrifying for Monica as her reality begins to blend with fiction, and something else entirely. . . some indescribable evil out in those woods.

"I had to read through my fingers...it was that scary for me."
- Scream Magazine on Tamer Animals

JUSTIN M. WOODWARD

ROTTEN LITTLE THINGS

A NOVELLA

56443731R00126

Made in the USA
Columbia, SC
25 April 2019